The Rescue
Of Fletcher Morgan

By

Gary D. Oliver

Oliver House Publishing

Copyright © 2005 by Gary D Oliver
All Rights Reserved
Gary D Oliver
Oliver House Publishing
#4 RD 2891
Aztec, New Mexico 87410
1-505-334-3209

Printed in the U.S.A. by
Morris Publishing
3212 E. Highway 30
Kearney, NE 68847
1-800-650-7888

Library of Congress Control Number 2006904828
ISBN # 0-9779031-0-9

To Daryl & Clarice Sutton — Oct 2006

DEDICATED TO
~Sugar~
My wife of 50 years

SPECIAL THANKS TO
Harry and Glenda Fassett
Anita Martinez
Amy Gillingham and
anyone else who had a
part in its production

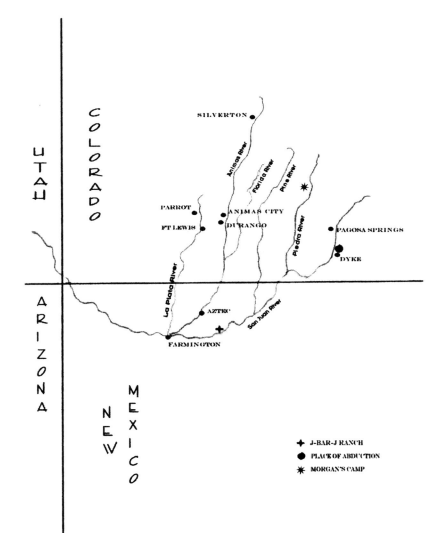

The Rescue of Fletcher Morgan

One

Fletcher Morgan loved the mountains. His passion for them went much deeper than just their natural beauty. More important to him was the feeling of freedom that engulfed him as he traveled through the valleys and over the mountain tops. There was a healing in the peace and tranquillity that was so bountiful in this mountainous world. And his troubled soul needed their soothing powers. This is not to say he wasn't fascinated and intrigued by the bountiful wealth and treasures that could be found here. He was. Now as a young man he spent most of his time pursuing everything they had to offer. Most of those who shared this mountainous wonderland with him were solely attracted by the precious metals they hoped would bring untold wealth and a life of leisure. While Fletcher was aware of these treasures and to some extent utilized them, it was those more important things that kept compelling him to live by the sometimes harsh rules of nature. He never dreamed that soon he would find a far greater treasure, right here in the San Juan Mountains of southwest Colorado.

The year was 1890. It was late August or maybe early September—it was hard for him to tell. After a good snowfall last winter, it had been an unusually hot and dry summer. But now it was raining almost every day, some storms being severe. He knew fall was coming, he could feel it in his bones. There was that something special in the air that had its own particular smell and feel. A feeling that heralded a change in the season. Even the melody of the wind, as it blew playfully through the drying Aspen leaves, was unique to this seasonal change. While it was still unusually warm during the day, the nights were starting to take on the chill that would eventually turn into the frost of fall, followed by the snows of winter.

He had been out since April. Leaving Durango, he had wandered up the Animas River to Silverton. After a short visit with some friends and making sure he had enough grub for the summer, he started back south along the eastern side of the river. Leaving the river, he had turned due east and worked his way towards the Continental Divide north of Pagosa Springs. He wasn't in a hurry. Leisurely he explored some of the streams that were plentiful in the area. Panning some for gold and, of course, indulging in one of the things that had brought him so much pleasure—fishing. He hadn't seen one human being. Except in late July. He had left the top of the Divide and gone down to Pagosa Springs since his supplies were running short and he needed to replenish them. He couldn't do without his coffee and the flour was getting low.

After a hot bath, shave, and haircut, Fletcher felt like a new man. In fact, he felt so good that he decided to stay the rest of the week and enjoy soaking in the hot mineral springs that Pagosa was famous for. Figuring he had enjoyed enough of the soft life, early one morning he packed up and left the comforts of civilized living. He headed out in a northwestern direction. The idea was to spend a couple of weeks at one of his old camp sites on the Piedra River.

After wandering around for about two weeks, he decided it was time to head for the Piedra or it was going to get too cold to enjoy this special camp. He topped a high ridge and was looking down on the Piedra River. While sitting there for a few minutes, taking in the panoramic view, something caught his attention. Way below and to the left was a Ute encampment. Close to the river, it was nestled in a grassy meadow between a small stream and a stand of quakies bordering the south. Being so far, it was hard to see what was going on. Reaching in his saddle bags, he pulled out an old spyglass his father had left him. It wasn't in the best shape, being scratched up some in the past, but it had served his purposes well enough. Quickly surveying the area he counted ten teepees. Several women were attending to their duties around the fires. A few kids and a dog or two were playing in the water. There were a couple of older men. Several ponies were tied in the Aspens but the camp was void of any boys or young men. This figured, since it was most likely a fall hunting camp. It was not uncommon for the Utes to leave the reservation in the fall to hunt elk and deer, a needed necessity if they were to survive the winter. There had been some talk in Pagosa Springs about some young renegade bucks engaging in some mischief and causing some trouble. There was some concern for the safety of the good citizens in and around Pagosa. In fact, a small detachment of soldiers had been sent from Fort Lewis to take care of the problem. Making a mental note of the situation, he turned his little group north and headed for his old camp, about seven or eight miles on up the river.

Those traveling with him included the dog, who wasn't very fond of people in general. He especially hated soldiers and Indians and avoided them if at all possible. He had been with Morgan since he was a pup. Morgan figured he was part wolf, being about that size and physically resembling one in shape and coloring. Then there was his horse, Blue. Morgan called him that because he was an odd colored dapple grey. With the growing of his winter coat, he took on a bluish hue. Finally, following close behind, came Millie, his snow white pack mare. That was good in some aspects since she had a tendency to wander at times and being white made her easy to find.

Upon reaching camp and setting up, he had done little else, except for a little fishing and dog paddling in some of the bigger holes of the river. Just this morning he had mused about how lucky he was—at least his life was peaceful and contented. But that was to end. Because then *she* came into his life.

****

On that particular day, Morgan and the dog had spent the day fishing and swimmng in the river that ran a few feet from their camp. It had rained some during the night so it had been a warm and muggy day. They had had an early supper and since it was getting late in the afternoon, the dog had found a sunny spot and settled down for a nap. Morgan was fixing to have a cup of coffee. Suddenly the ears of the dozing dog started twitching. Morgan caught the movement as he stooped to fill his cup from the pot sitting on the dying coals of the cook fire. Abruptly the dog raised his head, his ears straining to hear the faint sound. The hair bristled on his back and a low growl came rumbling up from deep in his chest.

"What is it, Dawg?" the man whispered. "Something bothering you, boy? Heck, I better take a look," he mumbled as he set the cup down. "Something's got him all excited."

Before he could stand up the dog had moved towards the rock out-cropping that hid their camp. Quickly following, scrambling up the slope and laying on his belly, he crawled to the edge, carefully separating the willows and foot high grass growing along the bluff side. Movement on the far side of the river caught his attention. Several riders were emerging from among the Aspens.

"Utes!" he muttered under his breath, as half a dozen of them cleared the trees and worked their way down towards the river. *Probably a hunting party,* was his first inclination.

It didn't take long to realize that that was a bad assessment. For one thing, they were all riding bareback and, except for the breech-cloths and moccasins, they were stark naked. As they got closer he could make out the faint, tell-tale markings of the yellow and black paint that Utes would smear on their bodies when making a raid. Besides, they were being very noisy and boisterous, as if celebrating some great victory. He was rolling these things over in his mind when they reached the river bank and headed north.

That's when he saw her.

"A white woman!" he gasped under his breath, a cold shiver running up his spine.

She was sitting in front of a young buck riding a big black pony. He was grasping a rifle in one hand and holding her with the other. She was slumped over and appeared unconscious, her long auburn hair covering most of her face. Her dress was torn and barely hung on her slender frame.

Sizing up the other riders, it wasn't hard to see what they had been up to. Each one of them had a rifle in one hand and a bottle of whiskey in the other, with several bottles tied across their ponies. They had been hunting, all right, but not for game.

A raiding party, he thought. *A bunch of renegades. I wonder if they are the same ones I was warned about in Pagosa?*

His biggest concern now was for the woman. He didn't know who she was or how they got her, but the lady was in a lot of trouble. As he watched them disappear around the bend in the river, he had a sickening feeling deep down in the pit of his stomach. He knew he had to do something, but at the moment he didn't know what.

"Well, Dawg," he said, as he slid back down the incline, "I guess it's up to us to get her out of her predicament. The Lord only knows what they have done to her, or will do."

All the horror stories that he had heard about white captives, especially the women, came flooding into his mind. The uneasy feeling was turning to anger as he thought of what she was enduring. The big question now was, how was he going to take her from them? He had a lot of respect for the Utes as warriors. He knew he couldn't just walk in and take her. He wasn't too keen on losing his hair, either, just to save a woman who was a total stranger. Maybe if he followed them, when they stopped for the night he could sneak in and rescue her without too much of a scuffle.

Grabbing the saddle blanket and saddle, without breaking his stride he headed for his horse. Sensing the presence of the Indian ponies, Blue and Millie had already come up near the camp. Blue was holding his head high, his ears straining forward, his nostrils flaring.

"Don't make a sound, you worthless horse," the man said quietly.

Quickly he laid the blanket on Blue's back and set the saddle in place, cinching it securely. After putting the bridle on, he reached for his gun belt, strapping it on. Then placing his worn carbine in its scabbard on the saddle, he was ready. Placing his boot in the stirrup, he started to swing up on Blue when it occurred to him that he had better tie Millie up. He couldn't afford to have her following them. She would only be in the way. Getting her halter rope, he soon had his pack horse securely tied to a small cottonwood growing close to the cliff side.

Returning to Blue and mounting with a single motion, he nudged the horse and they slipped through the narrow inlet of their camp into a large maze of willows that was flooded most of the year. Blue picked his way through the willows and headed across the river. The dog, reaching the other side ahead of them, wasted no time getting on the trail the renegades had left. Breaking into a trot, the horse and rider fell in behind, the man anxiously mulling over in his mind how he was going to pull off this rescue.

It was still an hour before dark. He thought it best to hang back until he knew exactly where the Indians were. The wind was picking up a little now. As the breeze blew against his face, he could feel and smell the moisture in the air that always preceded an oncoming storm. Huge black and purple thunderheads were rolling in from the northwest. The distant rumbling of thunder could be faintly heard. The bursts of light that signaled the presence of lightning were visible on the western horizon. The eerie darkness that was hastening the coming of night was closing in on them.

The storm, which promised to be a drencher, moved ever closer at a rapid pace. It wouldn't be long before lightning would be streaking across the ever-darkening sky, not only creating a panorama of zigzag patterns, but bringing with it the downpour of rain.

"Man, I hope it holds off for a spell," he muttered under his breath. "I hate getting wet."

It was getting dark now. A growl from the dog brought the rescuers to a halt. A few hundred yards ahead the flickering light of a small fire could be seen shining through the trees. Good, they had stopped for the night. If he was lucky, they would be getting good and drunk. He'd need all the help he could get.

Riding up as close as he dared, making sure he was downwind from the Indian ponies, he stopped. He tied the reins together, letting them hang over Blue's neck. That way he wouldn't have to hunt for them in case of a hasty retreat. Before dismounting, he took a quick reading of the tree line against the night sky, trying to fix the location in his mind, hoping he could find the spot again in the dark.

The dog had already taken off in the direction of the fire. Crouching down, the man followed as quietly as he could, carefully making his way through the tall grass and scattered willows. Soon he was just a few yards from the edge of the clearing. Crawling those last few feet on his belly, he eased up to the edge of the grass, pausing behind a small clump of willows to take a look and size up the situation. Before doing anything, he needed to finalize the plan that had been going through his mind for the last hour.

Their night camp was well chosen. A fire was built up against a rock cliff that jutted out at the top, affording good protection from the coming storm. Their ponies were tethered in a thick growth of pine trees just a few feet to the south. The woman was lying motionless about a dozen yards to the north of the fire, just inside the circle of light. Glancing back at the ponies, he could make out six of them in the dim glow of the fire.

An angry outburst brought his attention back to the fire. It was apparent that the young bucks were having a grand ol' time drinking what was left of the whiskey. It was also evident that there was a heated discussion going on. Four of them were sitting cross-legged around the fire. The one standing was waving his arms and yelling about something. Two of those sitting on the ground were loudly disagreeing with whatever it was that he was saying.

"Wait a minute!" the white man mumbled. "That's only five. Where's the other one?"

Going over everything in his mind again, he still came up with six ponies but only five Utes. He was sure there had been six when he had seem them earlier. *Where in the world is the other one?* He pondered for some moments. *I better hold on for a mite longer. I've got to know where that other heathen is.*

Studying the ones at the fire, it dawned on him that the missing one was the tall Ute who had been holding the woman. It crossed his mind that he was probably their leader and not as drunk as the rest. If so, it wasn't good news. But where could he be? The rescuer carefully reviewed everything once more. The missing man wasn't with the ponies and it was for sure he wasn't at the fire. *I sure hope he's on that side of the camp,* he thought, shaking his head. Crawling around the edge of the clearing, he worked his way closer and closer to the woman. His mind was still occupied with concerns about the missing Ute.

He didn't like the direction the talk at the fire was taking. He understood enough of the Ute lingo to know that they weren't too happy about the white woman being with them. From what he could make out, it was apparent that the one they called Two Bears was determined to take her as his woman. Some of the rest didn't like the idea and thought it was going to cause them a lot of trouble. They wanted to get rid of her.

He hated crawling around on the ground covered with weeds and stickers. But, most of all, he hated the little critters that were down on the ground with him—especially snakes. The thought of meeting up with one of them made his skin crawl. It was bad enough in the daylight, but in the dark....he tried to shake it from his mind.

Suddenly a cold chill ran down his spine. Something had touched his leg! As he whirled around, halfway expecting a snake or at the worst the missing hostile, the lightning lit up the sky and there stood the dog.

"For crying out loud," he muttered with a sigh of relief. "Dawg, you just shaved ten years off my miserable life!"

Taking a deep breath or two to get rid of the shakes, he gathered himself together again. He knew he didn't have much time and he needed a distraction.

Whispering to the dog, *"Look Dawg,"* as if he understood him, as somehow he always did, "when I give the word, pile into that bunch at the fire and I'll grab the woman."

As he crawled closer, he could hear her moan. That was good. At least she was still alive. Although it was hard to see in the faint light of the fire, it appeared that she was tied by one wrist to a small pine. He lay there for a few minutes, hoping the missing Indian would show up, but there was no sign of him. It would be raining soon and he didn't want to wait any longer.

"Go get 'em, boy," he commanded the dog.

In a flash the dog was across the clearing, landing smack in the middle of the arguing Indians. Running in a crouched position, the man got up behind the pine tree where the woman lay. With a quick slice of his knife, he cut the rawhide binding her. Kneeling, he carefully took her in his arms and she moaned again as he gently put her over his left shoulder. This way his shooting arm would be free to use Colt, if the need arose. Turning, he started in the direction of the waiting horse. There was quite a commotion going on in the vicinity of the fire. *Good*, he thought, *time to get out of here.*

He had only taken a half dozen steps, barely reaching the edge of the firelight, when he came face to face with the missing Ute.

"Lordy!" He cried out loud.

Instinctively doubling up his fist and without breaking stride, he swung at his foe just as hard as he could. The blow landed right in the middle of the surprised Redman's nose. The Ute went sprawling backward into the darkness, landing flat on his back. His rifle flew out of his hand, landing in the tall grass a few feet away. Wasting no time surveying the damage, the white man hurried to the spot where he thought the horse would be. It was pitch dark now and he couldn't see the tree tops so how was he going to find the horse?

"Blue," he called, "where are you?"

Just then the sky lit up and the ground shook as a bolt of lightning struck so close that it almost curled his hair. Straight ahead, just a dozen feet or so, was ol' Blue, patiently waiting for his passengers. But, thanks to the flash of light, the dazed and bloodied Indian saw his rifle and started for it. Still trying to clear his head, he grabbed the gun and cocked it, but the darkness engulfed them again and he lost sight of the white man.

Reaching the horse, the white man slid the woman off his shoulder and, as quickly and gently as he could, he laid her across the saddle. The scrapping and yelling was still going on at the fire. Then he heard a loud yelp. *Hope that dog is all right*, he thought. Grabbing the saddle horn and swinging up behind the saddle, he let out a shrill whistle, which was the dog's signal to come. On being nudged with the heel of his boot, the horse headed out at a quick pace.

At the sound of the whistle, the Ute fired a wild shot in the general direction of the noise. The only thing it hit was the pine tree that Blue had been standing under. In the darkness the white man was completely lost and didn't have the faintest idea which way was back to camp, but the horse did. As he started to make the turn that would take them to the river's edge and home, his hoof struck a rock. The Indian, picking up on the noise, blindly fired a shot in the direction of the departing horse. The man felt the burning sting of the bullet as it grazed the flesh of his upper left arm.

Riding a safe distance, he halted the horse, just as the dog, limping slightly, caught up with them. Taking stock of his arm, he realized his wound wasn't very serious. It wasn't bleeding much and would keep until they reached camp.

Repositioning the woman, he sat her up in the saddle. Putting his right arm around her waist, he firmly pulled her up against his chest. She would be more comfortable this way and holding her would be easier. She stirred as she regained consciousness.

"Who are you?" she faintly asked as her hand weakly grasped at his arm.

"Name's Morgan, ma'am. Fletcher Morgan. You're safe now

and we're on the way to my camp."

Leaning her head back against his shoulder, she lost consciousness once more. Giving Blue his head, they started for home. The storm was moving in with all its fury. Scattered drops of rain started to fall. Stopping the horse, Morgan slid back and untied the slicker he had been sitting on. Unfolding it, he carefully wrapped it around the woman, making sure it covered her head. He wanted to keep her as dry as possible. The rain was coming down harder now and in no time he was soaked. He hated being wet and it seemed as if they would never get to camp. Finally Blue dropped off the river bank and started across. Morgan knew they were about there.

"Take it easy, fella," the man commanded, as the horse started into the willows. Holding the slicker as tightly as he could around the woman, he let the horse work his way through the willows, slipping through the narrow opening leading to the camp. Morgan marveled at the unerring ability that a horse had for finding its way home, even in the dark.

Stopping in front of the camp, a combination of cave and cliff overhang which provided them adequate shelter, the horse waited to be relieved of his load. Steadying the woman, Morgan slipped to the ground, letting her slide off into his arms. Feeling his way into the shelter, he got her unwrapped from the slicker and, finding his bedroll, gently laid her on it.

By now it was a fierce cloudburst, streaks of lightning criss-crossing the sky and leaving an eerie glow in the night. The claps of thunder were so loud that the ground seemed to shake as the blowing rain hammered down on the earth. Considering the circumstances, it was very doubtful that there would be any pursuit by the Indians tonight. So he decided to take a chance and light the candle he kept sitting on a small rock ledge in the cave wall. Fumbling around in the dark, he found it and soon had it lit. The woman, regaining consciousness once more, blinked her eyes in the dim candlelight until she could finally focus them on Morgan.

"You're safe now, ma'am. Just lie still and you'll be all right."

"I'm so thirsty," she faintly whispered.

From the pail hanging at the rear of the cave, he filled a cup with fresh spring water. Returning, he knelt down beside her. Raising her head with one hand, he held the cup to her lips.

"Drink slowly," he said, as she started to gulp the water down. "Whoa, take it easy," he warned again. "Slow down. It's not good for you to drink too fast." When the cup was empty, she wanted more. "Okay," he answered, "but just a little."

After giving her a little more, he gently laid her head down with the assurance that he would give her some more later. Taking a damp cloth, he carefully cleaned the dirt and dried blood off her face. She flinched when he got to her wrists. They had been rubbed raw by the leather. Next he checked the cut on her ankle and found that it wasn't that serious—just a scrape. That would do for the night. He could tend to her wounds better in the daylight. Gently he helped her under the covers of the bedroll. Filling the cup, he let her drink some more.

"How are you feeling now?" he asked, as he finished tucking her in.

"I hurt all over," she sighed, "and I'm....*so* tired."

"You just close your eyes now and sleep. You're safe and I won't let anything happen to you."

The dog, who had been watching the goings-on with interest, moved over and laid down at her feet. Taking the candle, Morgan knelt by the animal, carefully checking to see if he had been seriously hurt in his scrimmage. All he found was a skinned place on his rib cage. Happily there were no broken bones. Relieved that the dog was all right, Morgan rolled up his sleeve and took a look at his own wound. It was just a scratch—nothing to worry about. Cleaning it out with some water, he found the salve and generously rubbed some on. Checking the woman once more and satisfied he could do no more until morning, he blew out the candle. Picking up his slicker, he slipped it on and went out to unsaddle Blue. Blue and Millie were huddled up between the cliff and a stand of cottonwood trees that provided a measure of protection from the downpour of rain.

"Easy, boy," he said, as he loosened the cinch and pulled the saddle and blanket off with his right hand. With his left, he reached up and slipped the bridle off. Blue shook himself briskly as the man put the saddle and bridle away. After turning Millie loose, he walked over to the opening of their hide-away and placed a pole across it.

Satisfied that all was buttoned up till morning, he sloshed back to the cave. Taking off the slicker and fumbling around in the dark, he found some dry clothes and changed. Slipping his old duster on to get warm, he sat down with his back against the rock wall and tried to get comfortable for the night.

Must be past midnight by now, he thought as he listened to the rhythmic sound of the falling rain. Although he had gotten soaking wet and was miserable, he was thankful it was raining so hard. It would make it hard for the Indians to track them in the morning. He didn't like the prospect of having to deal with six angry, wet, and hung-over Indians. But why worry about that now? He'd cross that creek when he came to it.

Man, what I wouldn't give for a cup of hot coffee right now, he thought wistfully and with that pleasant thought he settled down for the night. But he didn't get much sleep and the night dragged on as if it would never end. His arm ached and his fist was swollen and sore, especially when he tried to close it. He dozed off and on. Several times her cries would awaken him. The dog didn't have any trouble sleeping and lay by her feet without moving all night.

Two

When dawn came the rain was still falling, though it was only a drizzle now. There was a blanket of low-lying fog enveloping the trees and creeping slowly down the hillsides. As a whole, it made for a very dreary and depressing morning. The chill in the air on this late summer day didn't help his sore and stiff body either. His hand was still swollen and he grimaced as he opened and closed it. It took several times of working his fingers back and forth before they limbered up enough to be used. His left arm was a bit sore, a reminder of how close he came to being badly hurt. He shuddered to think what would have happened if he had sat the woman up in the saddle in the first place. The Indian's shot would have hit her for sure.

He forced himself up from the sitting position that he had slept in. As his aching body straightened, he uttered a moan or two and then after several steps everything started working again. He decided it was safe enough to build a small cook fire. The smoke would mingle with the fog. He'd have to take a chance on them smelling it. Taking some dry wood that he kept in the back of the shelter, he soon had one going.

He needed a cup of coffee in the worst way and he would need some warm water to clean up his guest. When she woke he would take care of her wounds and feed her some breakfast. Checking, he found she was still in a deep sleep. The dog, although awake, was still curled up at her feet.

The brewing coffee brought him back to life. It was like a bit of heaven when that first sip hit his lips and warmed his gut. The dog was watching his every move with keen interest. Raising his cup up to his lips for a second sip, he focused his gaze on the dog.

"Dawg, you just don't know what you're missing," he said with a sigh of contentment. "There's nothing in the world like a good cup of coffee on a morning like this." Then as an amusing afterthought, he added, "Hope them devils don't smell this brew or the fire. But, what the heck, they're probably holed up somewhere waiting for the rain to stop. Hopefully their horses broke loose during the ruckus last night and they're having to round them up this morning."

The thought of that put a smile on his face as he put a pail of water on to heat. It's a sure bet there won't be any tracks to follow when they begin looking for the woman. And if by chance they do get close, the dog would pick up on it. If that happened, he'd just have to handle it the best way he could.

He was starving so he hurriedly whipped up some biscuits and gravy. Dishing up a generous helping for himself, he poured the rest into the dog's dish, keeping a small portion for their guest. He and the dog ate in silence. At last, wiping up the last bit of gravy, he disposed of it with a hardy smack. It was amazing how a full belly and a warm drink could perk up a man's soul.

The woman was still asleep but he thought it best to wake her. He needed to get some food in her and then take care of her wounds. Pouring a warm cup of coffee, he knelt down by her side. Gently patting her cheek and whispering "Ma'am", he finally got her to open her eyes. Raising her head with is left hand, he helped her to drink some of the coffee.

"Feeling any better this morning?" he asked.

"No," she replied weakly. "I hurt all over."

After she had finished the coffee, he asked her if she would eat something, but before he could get an answer she fell asleep again. Laying her head down, he got a pan of warm soapy water and proceeded to clean her face and then her arms. Taking the salve, he rubbed a little on the scratches and cuts, especially her wrists where they were raw from being tied with the rawhide straps. Pulling the blankets back, he cleaned and dressed the gash on her ankle and he washed her feet. He then covered her up so she could rest. Since she was running a fever, he wet a small rag and laid it across her forehead. He looked down at her and saw how pale and translucent her face was. Before he could stop himself, he ran his fingers lightly over the side of her face. So soft—like a piece of velvet he'd seen at the mercantile store. It was perfect, except for a little scratch or two that marred the surface.

About mid-morning the rain stopped and the cloud cover started breaking up. Hopefully the sun would soon be out and warm things up. He thought it best to watch from his vantage point behind the willow cover. The rifle was propped up on the bank side where it would be handy if he needed it in a hurry. But it had been quiet and he hoped it would stay that way. The dog stayed close to the woman. He had made himself her official protector. While he didn't think much of the male gender, he felt comfortable with the ladies.

The heavy rain had swollen the river until it was almost over its banks. The muddy water had taken on a dark brownish color. There were all kinds of trash being swept along by its roaring torrent. He wasn't surprised to see a small tree or two float by. In the ripples just above the camp he could hear large rocks rolling on the bottom of the river bed. He was intrigued that water could move big rocks like that. It had been some rain, all right.

As the day wore on, the sky continued to clear until there were only a few small puffy white clouds lazily floating by now and then. The late summer sun was warming the earth, drying away the effects of nature's downpour of the night before. The water in the river was receding and beginning to clear.

Checking on the woman, Morgan found she was still asleep, so he resumed his place at the willow embankment. He needed to keep an eye on the other side of the river in case they had visitors. Leaning back in a comfortable position, his body started soaking up the warmth of the afternoon sun. As time dragged on, now and then he would catch himself dozing off. Suddenly the dog left his protective spot at the feet of his newly found friend. Hair bristling on his back, he edged up to where Morgan was napping. His growls alerted the man, a warning that someone was coming.

In a few moments he saw the movement of an Indian pony working its way through the brush along the river bank. A couple more riders were weaving their way along the hillside, their eyes focused on the ground. No doubt about it, they were looking for him and the woman.

In the lead was Morgan's newest enemy, the young buck who

had been holding the woman when Morgan first saw them, and there was no doubt that he was the one whom Morgan had hit on the nose last night. As the black horse came down to the water's edge, the Ute let him lower his head to drink. Looking out across the water it seemed as if he was staring straight at Morgan and the dog.

Don't look him in the eye, Morgan reminded himself.

As the Ute sat there letting his pony drink, it gave Morgan time to size up this worthy foe. He was unusually tall for a Ute, probably six-two, judging by sight and the experience Morgan had had with him the night before. His handsome features were marred by his swollen, broken nose. Two long jet black braids hung down each side of his face, resting on his chest. The ever-familiar yellow and black war paint was still evident on his dark brown muscular body.

One of his comrades rode up beside him and started what sounded like a heated discussion. Although Morgan listened as best he could, it was hard to understand everything because of the river noise. The fact that he didn't understand all the Ute language didn't help either. If Morgan had translated correctly, the tall one was called Two Bears. That was a strange name for a Ute, since they worshipped the bear and it was unlikely they would use the name. But still, that's what it sounded like. Could he have other blood in him, like Cheyenne? It didn't make any difference. Morgan decided to call him Two Bears anyway.

One fact was evident. Two Bears was determined to have the white woman. From what Morgan could hear, the Ute was fascinated with the color of her hair and especially her green eyes. Morgan had to admit that they did make for a beautiful combination. There was an added reason for the Ute to find them.

Morgan had humiliated the young warrior by stealing the woman, especially in front of his cohorts. On top of that, he had hit him in the face, which the Indian would have taken as an insult.

Two Bears was uneasy. His gaze kept returning to the far side of the river, but Morgan knew he couldn't attempt to cross here. Between Morgan and Two Bears the river made a long, gradual bend that formed a long, wide and deep slow-moving pool of water. From where the Ute sat, it looked as if the river was running up against the bluff and gave the appearance of blending into the mountainous cliff behind it. Besides, with the water still being high and considering all the trash, it would be doubtful that the Indian would attempt to cross.

Morgan's camp and the little meadow where Blue and Millie were kept was hidden from any who might be standing on the east side of the river. It was like nature had built a fort. The entrance was well hidden, too. To get into their hideaway, one would have to cross at the bend just above the ripples about five hundred yards to the north. It would then be necessary to work their way through a large stand of willows and grass growing in a swampy marsh. On top of that, one would have to know exactly where the small hidden entrance to the camp was. The only other way in was where the small stream that came down through the little meadow emptied into the river a few feet from where Morgan now lay. This, too, was well hidden by a huge rock that jutted out into the pool. To get to this spot a person would have to swim.

The fact that it was so well hidden and hard to access made the site desirable. Especially if you didn't want anyone to know you were in the neighborhood. But then again, the thought had crossed his mind that the Indians just might know about it, too.

Two Bears started pacing up and down the river bank. For some reason he was unsure of the circumstances and was carefully looking for any indication of the white man's presence. Morgan grasped his rifle, putting his thumb on the hammer.

"He'll be one sorry Indian if he does decide to come," Morgan whispered to the dog, though it was doubtful that the dog heard him above the river noise. The dog would probably welcome the opportunity to get a bite of the man that, by circumstances, he hated. For a good fifteen minutes the Ute stared at the bluff, trying to detect some movement that might explain the uneasiness that he couldn't shake. He knew he wanted the woman back and had a feeling she was near. He wouldn't stop until he had her.

Evidently deciding there was nothing unusual along the bluff, he motioned to the others who had been impatiently waiting for him to move on. Turning their horses downstream, they soon disappeared from Morgan's view. Morgan knew they wouldn't give up easily and that they'd continue to look for signs that would lead them to the man who had stolen their leader's prize.

He released the hammer on his rifle, breathing a sigh of relief as he returned to check on the sleeping woman. After being assured that she was all right, he fixed himself a more comfortable place to sleep. Stretching out on his blanket and putting both hands on the back of his head, he figured it was a good time to relax and try to sort things out. He couldn't shake the uneasy feeling deep in his gut—the feeling that they hadn't seen the last of Two Bears.

What kind of man is he? he wondered. *Maybe I'll never know.* But he knew that wasn't likely as he dozed off.

****

Two Bears, among other things was a stubborn man. He was

persistent as well. As a general rule he pursued the thing he wanted until he got it. Another thing that made him dangerous was his immense pride. Pride in his heritage and the ancestral home of his people. He resented the white man for intruding into his world and, in effect, changing it into something foreign to the sacred ways of the Utes. To the white man he was a renegade, but to the Utes way of life he was a patriot. He was only six years old when his father was gravely wounded in a scrimmage with a band of buffalo hunters. After three days of suffering he died. Because of this and other injustices that he had witnessed at the hands of the white intruders, his resentment had grown into hatred and rebellion.

The product of a mixed union, a Cheyenne chieftain and a Ute maiden, he was taller and more muscular than most of his Ute companions. One fall the Cheyenne had raided a small band of Utes picking piñon nuts in the foothills of southwestern Colorado. As his war party charged the main group, Big Bear, Two Bear's father, and a companion made off with two young women who had wandered off from the others. On the way back to the plains, he decided to take the pretty one as a wife. He treated her well and she came to love him. But he knew she missed her home in the mountains and yearned to return.

In the first six summers of his life, Two Bears learned much about the Cheyenne way of life and their language. In addition, his mother saw to it that he also learned of her former way of life with the Utes. When the buffalo hunters shot Big Bear and he knew he was dying, he made his brothers promise to return Grey Owl and her son to her home land.

Back with the Utes, he was raised with the family of his mother. It wasn't easy on young Two Bears. He had a new language to master and new customs to adjust to. Besides that, there was the abuse inflicted by the other children because of his being half Cheyenne. After several altercations, he established himself as a leader and earned the respect of his peers. The circumstances in his life sufficed to make him strong and determined.

The father of Grey Owl, who was getting along in years, had taken an immediate liking to his new grandson. He taught Two Bears well—how to hunt and the fine art of making war. There was much to learn if he was to survive in the wilderness and Two Bears was an eager student. He learned well the ways of the creatures of the forest. He mastered the art of becoming one with them and the land on which they all lived. He developed into a superb horseman and was apt in the techinque of counting coup— striking a living enemy with his hand, weapon, or coupstick. He did well in borrowing things from the Spanish and Mexicans who had settled that part of the southwest. He figured he should treat the white man the same way but had been branded a renegade.

In the winter time the snow blowing and howling around their teepee chilled the earth, turning it harder than stone. The little family group would huddle in their robes around a small open fire and listen by the hour to Grandfather telling stories of the old way of life. He described the times before the Spanish and Whites had come, changing the old ways of the Indian. Then he told how the Utes stole and traded for horses from the Spanish. These horses made them fierce and feared warriors of the mountains. His young mind was filled with the experiences of raids and battles fought for fame and plunder. After the storytelling was over and everyone had settled down for the night, he snuggled down under his robes and relived in dreams the glory days of his people and nurtured his hatred for the ones who were bringing it all to an end. So it was not only his personal experiences in life that had poisoned his mind against the white invaders, but his grandfather had fed that strong emotion of hatred. The old man had constantly beat into the heart of Two Bears that to trust them was foolish, as they were the enemy.

Once when Two Bears was about fifteen years old, he asked Grandfather if all white men were evil. He was told that there were a few good ones—that some had treated the Utes and their ways with respect—but most were greedy and cruel and cared little for the land that nourished them. A few years later the old man softened some toward the whites. Two Bears had been up north running with some troublemakers, getting into all kinds of mischief. There had been several flare-ups along eastern Colorado and a major one to the north, the Meeker massacre. This had brought the Utes into conflict with the U.S. Army. Two Bears and five or six of his companions were involved in some of these battles. When he returned south he learned that his Grandfather had been saved from certain death by a white man. He had been attacked by two white prospectors, who had almost beaten him to death. A young white man had happened along and killed the two men and saved the old Indian. This man nursed him back to health and took care of him until he was found by several cousins of Two Bears. He had thanked this kind man by giving him a special pony as a gift. This pony was an odd-colored one. Looked like the dark blue of the thunder clouds. He had asked his people not to harm the young man with the blue horse. He said that this white man had the spirit of a true warrior.

Then one late afternoon when Two Bears and his band of renegades rode into Dyke to trade for supplies, things went wrong. When the trader had refused to give them whiskey, there was a big argument and the Indians were told to leave. They mounted their ponies and left. This was done under the watchful eye of Mr. Summers and an employee who was pointing a rifle in their general direction. Just then the stage came limping in with a damaged wheel and Two Bears saw the woman. He decided there and then that he was going to have her for his own. That night, a short distance from Dyke, they sang and danced, stripping down and painting their bodies for a raid on the station the next morning. Just as the repaired stage was being loaded for the trip on to Pagosa Springs, they struck. After the smoke cleared and two men were lying on the ground, Two Bears grabbed his prize and took off. Taking as much whiskey as they could find, the others lit out after him. Now the woman had been stolen from *him*, by a white man. He was boiling with rage as they searched.

****

Back up the river, the rest of the day passed without incident. Morgan decided on a cold camp that night, although he would miss his hot coffee. After eating a couple of cold biscuits and some leftover beans, he woke the woman. But all he could get her to do was drink some water, then she immediately returned to sleep.

He wasn't about to spend another night like the night before, so he rigged up a more comfortable place to sleep. Even though it was the latter part of summer, it still got chilly in the wee hours of the morning. He'd let the woman have the use of all his blankets, so he'd have to make do with his old duster and the saddle blanket as covers. It wasn't the best, especially the smelly blanket, but it would work in a pinch.

The sun had set and evening was settling in as he sat looking at the woman.

She is a beautiful lady, he thought. Some color had returned to her face and her dark, rich auburn hair had fallen randomly across the pillow, a curl across her forehead. Although she was asleep he could still see those green eyes looking up at him. In the fading light she looked just like he imagined an angel might look.

As the last light of day slowly faded away, he sat in the stillness of the twilight listening to all the familiar sounds of the mountains. In the distance he could hear the cooing of the doves, a mournful call that echoed through the trees. The frogs in the willow-filled marsh started their nightly chorus, joyfully joined by some nearby crickets. He could hear the occasional flip-flop of the big river trout as they went about their nightly feeding. There was a serenity about this time of day that he would never get tired of. Being in the mountains beautified all the wonders of nature.

Yes, there wasn't any doubt that the mountains were in Fletcher Morgan's blood. As long as he could remember, he had been drawn to them and felt he belonged to them. As he sat there in the solitude of his little world, his mind went back to when he was a young lad living on the plains just north of his native Denver. He would sit in the swing on the front porch and stare off in to the distance at the towering peaks of the Rocky Mountains. He would close his eyes and as he daydreamed he could see himself there. Romping through the green meadows, playing or fishing in the many streams, climbing over the rocks that covered the hillsides, or gazing out at the magnificent displays of nature from some high vantage point. As he dreamed, he could hear the many wonderful sounds of the wilderness, the wind weaving its way through the trees, producing sweet and pleasant melodies as it played in the leaves and the cheerful songs of various birds that infested every part of that wonderful world. One of his favorites was the bugling of the bull elk at mating time, the vibrations of their call echoing through the canyons and up the mountainsides. He smiled as he thought of lying in his bedroll in the stillness of a clear night, staring up at the starry heavens and trying to count the stars as he listened to the howling of the coyotes in the meadow below.

He would never forget the multitudes of smells either. It seemed like there were a million different flowers, of all shapes, sizes, and colors that would blanket the slopes and meadows from early spring through late fall. Or the smell of wet earth after an afternoon shower in mid-summer. How he loved those mountain showers, the majestic power that the black thunderclouds displayed as they billowed in over the mountain tops. As the sky darkened and the flashing streaks of lightning cast eerie silhouettes across the rugged terrain, he would actually shiver with excitement and apprehension. How one would have to run for cover or be soaked to the bone and after the downpour, how clean and fresh the air smelled as you took in deep calming breaths. Then to feel the warmth of the emerging sun that would embrace the earth once more.

There were also the delicacies of the wild. Raspberries and alpine strawberries that you could munch on as you walked through this wonderland of the Creator. The chokecherries that could be cooked and used as preserves. The nuts of the piñon trees, appreciated not only by the little creatures, but also by man who could use them for food.

The many rivers and streams held a special place in Morgan's heart. There was nothing more enjoyable than to walk up or down one of these waterways. Whether one was fishing or just exploring, one couldn't help listening to the music of the water as it ran over the rocks and boulders. Watching the Dippers going about their business as they fed for the day or a mountain trout taking a fly from the surface of the water. At certain times of the day the light from the sun would hit the rushing water just right, causing it to sparkle like a million diamonds. Some of these streams held the riches that men dreamed of—yellow gold. Yes, there were many treasures of different kinds in those mountains and Fletcher Morgan loved them all.

Some of the fondest memories he had were of those rare occasions when his father would take the family up into the mountains for a few days. But those visits were brief and would end all too soon and they would return to the city. Fletcher came by his passion for the mountains honestly. His father, Clay, also had deep feelings for them. It had been his dream to move out of Denver to some small town in the mountains where a blacksmith was needed. There he could take care of his family and at the same time be close to the land he loved. Many times he had discussed his dream with his wife, Mary. She had been raised in the east. Being a refined lady, she was happy to stay in the city teaching children, which was the love of her life. But she had consented to go where Clay wanted to go and, as she told him often, there would always be children to teach—ones she could help learn to read and write and in that way enrich their lives.

When Clay heard about the rugged San Juan Mountains in southwestern Colorado, that this was a new country that people of adventure were streaming to by the thousands, he couldn't resist the urge to go see it for himself. Would this be the answer to his life-long dream? The stories told of riches beyond compare, of gold and silver there for the taking. Of mines that would be dug and towns that would be built. Lands in the lower elevations that were perfect for farming and the raising of cattle. So in the late spring of 1873, Clay, accompanied by Fletcher, who at that time was a lad of thirteen, headed for the mountains of southwest Colorado.

After spending some time in the higher mountains around what was to become Silverton, Clay decided to follow the Animas River south and see what the lower country had to offer. As they came to the place where the river leveled out, he knew this was the spot where he wanted to live. It was a beautiful long valley with fertile bottomland guarded by reddish cliffs of stone on both sides. At the south end of this valley was a farming and ranching community that was in the process of being born and nurtured. A little town that promised to become a trade center.

Clay liked this area because, unlike the higher ranges, the winters here were milder. Here was a place he could raise his family and be a part of history by helping a brand new community grow. They would need a blacksmith for sure. Clay and Fletcher stayed about a week, scouting the surrounding area, and the more they saw the better they liked it. Returning to Denver, Clay was determined to move his family to Animas City come next spring.

In the spring of 1874, after selling their home and business and saying good-bye to their many friends, Mary, Clay and their two boys were on their way south. After an extremely hard trip over the Continental Divide, which took several weeks, they arrived in the Animas Valley. Acquiring a parcel of land, the Morgan family spent the next year building a house and then a place to house the blacksmith shop. Finally in 1875 Clay Morgan was busy doing the thing he loved, being a smithy. Mary had also found her niche in the new community and was finding children she could teach to read and write.

Now in the year of 1890, they were gone and Fletcher had been on his own for the last ten years. He had grown into a man who stood six foot two, weighing nearly two hundred pounds. Light amber eyes complemented his dark brown hair. He preferred to be clean shaven and kept his hair fairly short. He was a solid, muscular man who had inherited the physical strength of his father, but the heart of his mother. He wore a chin strap on his hat so he could let it hang down his back. He loved to feel the wind blowing through his hair.

He wore a six gun on his right hip and he was very proficient in its use. There was a 30-30 carbine nestled in a scabbard on his saddle and he had become very handy with it, too. He had lived a bit in the last ten years and the school of hard knocks had taught him many a painful lesson, causing him to question in his mind what was important in life.

The mission in life that he felt compelled to follow started ten years ago. First it took him to the dry, flat country in New Mexico, Arizona, and Texas. Once he even found himself south of the border in Old Mexico. This part of his life lasted two years and he was ready to return home to his favorite country, the area around Animas City, Colorado. The next few years found him working out in his beloved mountains, first for the miners and then the Army. When leaving this behind, he had spent the last few years just roaming in what he figured was his domain. He spent the warmer months in the high country and the colder ones in the lower foothills of southwestern Colorado and northwestern New Mexico. This area, called the Land of the Six Rivers, covered almost ten thousand square miles and was truly his home.

Morgan felt it offered everything that was needed to make a man happy. There were extremely high and rugged mountain peaks and canyons so deep and rugged that only mountain goats could climb in and out of them. These graduated into the gentler foothills where the cedars, piñons, and oak brush flourished and where rich, flat farm lands could be found. So he felt his home offered abundant treasures for whatever a man wanted in his life. Whether it was connected in some way to the silver and gold mining, being a storekeeper, or some other service necessary for life—such as a farmer or rancher or just a drifter as he was—there were riches here for the taking.

A variety of people had been attracted to this world of Morgan's. For the most part, the natural beauty was not the treasure that they were seeking. It was the gold and silver. The dreams of striking it rich drove them to endure the severest of hardships and the very real threat of losing their lives. They came, trying desperately to satisfy the greed that motivated their very being.

The miners were the first to forge their way into these mountains, hoping to be the ones who discovered the mother lode and reaped the untold wealth that was hidden in the rugged terrain of the San Juans. Then came the farmers and ranchers, determined to reap some of the riches the miners would produce. They would do this by providing food and other necessities of life. Thus there came to be a need for merchants, traders, and suppliers of all kinds of goods, and so a commercial world was born.

At first it was just the men who braved the new frontier, but soon the women followed, the first being the *Ladies of the Night*. Then came the wives and sweethearts, who were to become the partners of those working men. It was a hard life. To be tamed, the land demanded much.

Man had to find ways of conquering this wilderness in order to bring out its precious contents. He had to conquer the bitter cold and the deep snow that the winters brought, snow so deep it almost stopped the movements of men and their equipment. Even in the lower regions the winters, while milder, were still hard to contend with. It took long days of hard work to tame this wilderness, to build homes and businesses and all the necessary things to make life possible.

And so, a special breed of people came, ones who were determined and willing to take on the severe task of surviving and making it work. Sadly, there were also the leaches and dredges of society that flooded into the land to live off the sweat and tears of others. Among them were the ladies of the night who were ready and willing to sell their bodies, relieving stupid men of their hard-earned money. There were the saloon keepers and gamblers who supplied abundant amounts of liquor and games of chance, thus giving the unwary the opportunity of sacrificing to the god of good luck. Not to be overlooked were those who were outright thieves, who, by force, would relieve honest folks of their valuables. Because of the lawless elements and the lack of law enforcement, the early years were hard and dangerous ones.

Suddenly it dawned on Morgan that he had been daydreaming again. It was well after dark now and he was tired. Checking on his patient once more, he made sure she was covered and all tucked in for the night. Returning to his own makeshift bedroll, he made himself as comfortable as possible.

As he lay there, staring up at the starry heavens, he couldn't get the girl out of his mind. Who was she? Where was she from? What kind of person was she? Did she have family—a husband, children? If she did they surely would be sick with worry. How in the world did she get into this awful mess?

Well, maybe tomorrow he'd get some answers. With that thought he drifted off to sleep.

Three

It hadn't been a good week for J.J. Jackson. He had sprained his ankle so badly that he could hardly bear to walk on it. His leg was black and blue clean up to the knee. Now the marshal from Aztec was telling him that his daughter had been kidnapped from the stage stop at Dyke and they didn't know where she was. This last bit of news hit him hard.

"When did this happen?" he demanded. "Who would do such a thing?"

"Yesterday. It was about half a dozen Utes," replied the marshal. "We think they're part of the renegades that's been causing some trouble the last few months. They hurt several men pretty bad, in fact a couple of them may not make it. After looting the place they took off with Roseanna. The army has sent some soldiers to go after them."

Dumbfounded, J.J. slumped down in his chair. All the color

had drained from his face. His wife was pacing the floor, crying and wringing her hands. Finally, as if talking to himself, Jackson spoke. "I'll send someone up to the north pasture and get Brad." Then, after a pause, he spoke to the lawman. "Marshal, would you mind going by Larry's place on your way back to Aztec? Tell him the situation and ask him to come over here as soon as he can. And thanks for coming and telling us so soon."

"I'd be glad to. Try not to worry too much. She'll be all right. We'll get her back. Mornin', ma'am," the marshal said as he slipped on his hat and left the house.

"I hope so," the elderly man said, his voice betraying his deep concern for his daughter. "What would we do without her? There's one thing for sure," he said as he stood up, clenching his fist and gritting his teeth. "If they hurt her, there's going to be hell to pay—yes, sir, that's a promise."

J.J. Jackson was a man of his word. He had worked hard for what was his and even harder to keep it. He wasn't about to let anyone take any of it away, even if it took every ounce of strength he had to prevent it. He was a tall, lanky man. The wear and tear on his body caused him to stoop when he walked. His legs were slightly bowed and it was apparent that the long hard years of life had taken their toll. His hands and face were weathered by the wind and cold, the sun had turned them a dark brown like tanned leather. He sported a small, well-trimmed mustache that turned up on the ends. He wore his hair short, which he covered with an old wide brim hat that looked like it had been around for the full sixty summers of his life. His wife, Sunny, as she was called by everyone, was a good-natured sort of person with an upbeat attitude about life. Generally she was always humming some song, always with a smile on her face, always finding something in a situation to laugh about. She was of medium height and stoutly built, her long brown hair, which she usually wore in two braids, had started to gray at the temples.

Ever since she had teamed up with Mr. Jackson, as she had always called him, she had worked hard in helping to build the ranch and make it what it was today. She always supported him in the things he decided to do. Although he had never told her, she knew he appreciated the part she was playing in making the ranch a success. It had been a hard life, yet she found a lot of joy and contentment in it. But on this day, all the happiness she had known was gone and the thought of her little girl in the hands of savages was more than she could bear.

****

Brad was looking for strays in the north pasture when the rider caught up with him. When he heard the news, he did a bit of swearing, which was not unusual for him. Leaving the rider the task of bringing in the cattle, he lit out for the ranch house.

He was a man in his late thirties and was a lot like his father. He was as tall as J.J. and several pounds heavier. He was a hard man, not only physically, but emotionally too, the exception being his little sister. She touched a soft spot in his heart. He was a ruggedly handsome sort of man. He wore his hair fairly long and most of the time he had several days growth of stubble on his face. He had never shown any interest in getting married and raising a family. It seemed that all he wanted to do was work the ranch. Now that his father was getting older, he carried a heavier part of the load. Someday, as he figured it, the ranch would be his and he wanted it to be the best.

On the other hand, his younger brother, Larry, was completely opposite. As far as personality was concerned, he took after his mother. Larry was a shorter man, stocky in stature and was a friendly, outgoing person. Like his mother, he had a happy, optimistic outlook toward life. He was determined to make it on his own, so his father had loaned him the money and he bought a small farm. He had married a girl he'd known most of his life and they had three children, two girls and one boy. His farm was located down the San Juan River about fifteen miles from the J bar J Ranch.

Despite their differences, there was one thing the Jackson family agreed on and that was their love for the youngest, Roseanna. She had been something special from the very day of her birth. She was twelve years younger than Brad, who was four years older than Larry. She had played a lot with Larry. He was easy-going and they had a good time growing up. But it was Brad who had been her protector, the big brother she looked up to, the one she always felt secure with.

Now, as three of the Jacksons sat in the kitchen of the ranch house waiting for Larry to arrive, their thoughts were on Roseanna and there was agony in their hearts. J.J. got up from the table, hobbled over to the cookstove and poured himself a cup of coffee. He broke the silence as he sat down again.

"Remember the day she was born? She was so tiny and sickly that none of us thought she would make it."

"I remember," Sunny replied sadly, wiping a tear from her swollen eyes.

It was true. Roseanna had come into the world before she was ready. Sunny had taken a spill and it wasn't long after that that little Rose was born. Being premature, she suffered several difficulties, but thanks to an old country doc and the loving care of her mother, she pulled through. Then when she was a little older she had suffered a bout with rheumatic fever. Although she survived, it had left her weak and limited as to what she could do.

Because of her limitations, the whole family had become very protective of her. She always did what she could, but nobody expected much from her. She liked the outdoors and was proud of her flower garden that the family had helped her with, especially the wild rose bushes she tenderly cultivated around the fence of the yard. She would spend hours taking care of them or just sitting in the shade of the old willow tree looking at them. Even with the beauty of form and personality she possessed, few young men had pursued her for marriage. Most were looking for strong women who could carry a heavy work load and responsibility in the family. Besides, a suitor would have to go through Brad, which wouldn't be easy because nobody was good enough for his little sister. So she had remained single, but she never complained about her lot in life and did the best she could.

"Mr. Jackson," Sunny asked, as she put her arm around her husband's shoulder, "is she strong enough to survive such harsh treatment?"

"I just don't know," he replied, shaking his head. "She's emotionally strong and has a strong will to live. Maybe that will be enough, I just don't know."

Larry arrived later that evening with his family. "What are we going to do about this?" were the first words out of his mouth.

"First, we're going to settle down," J.J. said sternly, "and calmly discuss it."

"Look, Dad," Brad interrupted emphatically, "there's not much to discuss. It's for sure you can't go looking for her with your leg the way it is. That means I'll go!"

"Not without me, you won't!" Larry responded.

"But Larry," interjected Missy, Larry's wife, "what about the farm? It's harvest time and the crops can't wait."

"Hang the crops, honey, it's Rosie we're talking about and I'm going!" Then he turned back to his father. "Look, Dad, could you send one of your hands back with Missy so they can help with things until I get back?"

"That's no problem," the older man replied. "But it's not right for me to sit here and do nothing." Pure frustration showed all over the aging rancher's face. He couldn't get used to being in such a helpless situation.

"Right or not, Dad," Brad emphasized, "that's the way it's got to be. You can't ride in the shape you're in and, besides, you would only slow us down. We need to get there before the trail gets cold. You'll be needed here, to keep things lined out at this end."

J.J. knew his son was right. "Okay," he mumbled reluctantly, "but take Joe with you. He's handy with a gun. Your mother will fix enough grub to get you to Pagosa Springs." Getting out of his chair, this time he hobbled over to the pail setting on the cabinet and dipped out a cool glass of water. Turning his back to his oldest son, he added, "Each one of you will need to take an extra horse. That way you can change off and won't be killing the animals."

As Brad watched his father drink the water he felt the helplessness the older man was feeling in trying to cope with the situation.

"You got it," Brad replied, getting up out of his chair. "I'll go get the horses ready and tell Joe. Larry, you gather up the rifles, bedrolls and other things we'll need. Make sure we have plenty of ammunition. We'll be leaving before daylight," he added as he shut the kitchen door behind him.

Nobody slept much that night. Just as the eastern sky was starting to lighten up, they were all packed and ready to go.

"Boys," J.J. said as they were mounting up. "Last night your mother and I decided to offer a reward of a thousand dollars to anyone finding and returning Roseanna. Spread the word around when you get to Pagosa. We're hoping it will get a lot of folks looking for her. I'm going to send a rider to town to tell the marshall, too."

"Do you think that's wise?" Larry inquired. "It'll attract all the scum in the country."

"You may be right," his Dad replied, "but we have to try everything we can to get her back. Please, boys, humor us on this."

"Please be careful," their mother pleaded. "We don't want you boys getting hurt....or *worse*!"

Waving a final good-bye, the group headed toward the San Juan River, which they would follow to Pagosa Springs, Colorado. The San Juan River head watered on the east slope of the Continental Divide in southern Colorado. It angled off in a southwesterly direction, crossing over into New Mexico and then turning towards the west on its way to meet up with the Colorado River. The small town of Pagosa Springs was an important settlement near its headwaters. This spot on the river had been popular long before the white man appeared on the scene. There were several hot mineral springs here and the Indian people attributed medicinal properties to the water boiling up out of the ground. In fact, the word *pagosa* is Ute, meaning *healing waters* or *beaver*.

For years the Utes and Navajos had fought over these springs. After one such battle, they decided to choose a champion, one from each tribe to wage a single-handed fight, the winner having sole ownership of the area. The Navajos chose a large warrior to represent them and the Utes chose a white man to be their champion. The end result was that the Utes gained sole ownership of the hot springs from a well-aimed toss of the chosen weapon, a hunting knife. The Navajos never returned to the springs after that.

The Utes ownership was short lived, however, as a treaty with the U.S. government forced them out of that area and the white man moved right in to take advantage of the natural resources Pagosa Springs offered. Due to difficulties with the Utes, the Army decided to bring a garrison of soldiers into the area and so Fort Lewis came to Pagosa in the fall of 1878 and remained there for two years. The springs had become a popular place for visitors to come and bathe in the hot mineral waters. Roseanna Jackson was on her way to this small community to visit a friend when she was kidnapped at the stage stop at Dyke.

Her brothers arrived in Dyke the following afternoon. They talked to Mrs. Summers, the wife of the injured manager, and found out what she knew about the taking of their sister. She described as best she could the tall Ute riding a big black pony. She also mentioned that some of the soldiers and several scouts had left from the station the day of the kidnapping and were attempting to track the hostiles.

Later that night when the Jacksons reached Pagosa, they learned that a rider from the army had returned with the news of the thunder storm that had wiped out the trail of the kidnappers. He also told them that they had found a fresh trail of several horses and that they were following it. Brad hired this fellow to go with them and show them what the posse had found. They left Pagosa early the next morning, determined to find Roseanna. Ironically, these four riders passed within two miles of where Roseanna was being cared for by Fletcher Morgan. When they reached the spot where the posse had picked up the fresh tracks, they fell in behind, heading in a northeastern direction, taking them farther and farther away from their sister.

Four

About midnight Morgan was suddenly awakened by a clap of thunder. In a few minutes it was pouring down rain, another good old mountain cloud burst. Getting up, he checked his guest to be sure she was covered. She was sleeping like a baby. Lying back down, he was soon lulled to sleep by the relaxing rhythm of the rain. It poured for about thirty minutes then, as fast as it started, it stopped.

In the stillness of the dawning day, he awoke. For a while he lay there taking in the sounds and smells of a beautiful new morning. The sun would be up soon and the earth would be steaming as the moisture from the night before was dried by the warming air. Birds in the nearby willow marsh were singing their usual cheerful songs. As he gazed into a sky that was clear and bright, he could smell and feel the freshness of the newly washed earth. It was going to be a good day, he could feel it in his bones.

Building a small fire, he got the coffee started. The dog was gone, probably out hunting or maybe just checking things out. A quick trip around the meadow showed everything peaceful and quiet. Blue and Millie were milling around in front of the camp, curiosity had them checking out the newest member of the family. When Morgan got back, the coffee was ready and, pouring a cup, he sat back and relaxed. He would fix breakfast later after the woman woke up. He sat there for a moment looking at the young woman as she peacefully slept. He wondered how long it would be before she would be strong enough for the ride out. It didn't matter. They had plenty of food. He had planned to be out until the early snows, so even with an extra mouth to feed there would be plenty.

He was far from being a doctor but he had seen a lot of sickness and it seemed to him that this woman was not in the best of health. Her face was wan and pale, almost ghost-like, and she was still running a fever. It would be a spell for sure, he thought, before she would be able to take the stress of a ride home.

It must have been close to noon when the woman woke from her sleep, sat up and stretched. By now the fire was only embers but the coffee was hot and he had a pail of warm water ready. He had heated up the beans from the day before and had whipped up some biscuits and gravy.

"Well, good morning!" he said, pouring her a cup of coffee. "Feeling better today?"

"Not much," she replied, yawning as she pushed her hair back out of her face.

"By the way," he commented as he set the pot back on the hot ashes and handed her the cup. "I don't think I caught your name yesterday."

"It's Roseanna," she said softly, taking the cup out of his hand, "but most people call me Rose. I think you told me yours, but I can't seem to remember it."

"Fletcher Morgan, ma'am, and most folks just call me Morgan. Glad to meet ya," he said, shaking her hand. "Now that we know each other, would you like something to eat? Food's not much, just camp grub, but I think it's good, although some have disagreed with that assessment. One thing for sure, it'll keep a body alive."

"I don't know," she replied. "I don't feel much like eating. I'm so tired and I ache all over. But I would like a drink of water." With that, she set the coffee down beside her.

"Okay, but you'll need more than water," he said, handing her the water. I'll fix you a plate. You'll feel better after you've got something in your stomach. It would be good if you'd drink that coffee, too. It'll warm up your insides."

After finishing her water, she picked up the plate and ate a few bites then, setting it down, she picked up the cup of coffee and started sipping on it. "I feel so dirty," she murmured, as she finished up the last bit in her cup.

Morgan got the bar of soap, grabbed a towel and the pail of warm water and set them by her bed. Excusing himself, he went out to check on the horses. When he returned, he shook his head. She hadn't found the strength to clean herself. Instead she had snuggled down in the bedroll and was sound asleep.

He and the dog spent the rest of the day sitting at their spot in the willows. It was a warm, lazy afternoon and while listening to the hypnotic sound of the running water, he caught himself dozing now and then. He had half-way expected the Utes to return. He was positive the big one had suspected something and he couldn't understand why they hadn't come back for a second look. Could be they ran into some kind of trouble and had been sidetracked.

He woke the woman about an hour before dark. Her fever was down a little, her bruises and cuts were looking better. She drank a couple of cups of water and ate a biscuit with some gravy on it, finishing up with about half a cup of coffee. Before he could find out anything about her, she drifted off to sleep again. Cleaning up the camp for the day, he crawled into his bedroll. When he got up the next morning the dog was gone.

Probably tired of my cooking, he thought, *and is out hunting some grub of his own. Well, he needs the exercise anyway.*

Going down to the stream, he washed and shaved several days stubble off his face. When he was finished he got the morning chores done. The dog returned about the time Roseanna started stirring and he immediately went to eating the biscuits and gravy Morgan had set out for him.

"Breakfast is ready," Morgan said cheerfully to Rose. "How's our patient this fine morning?"

"Better, I think," she said, yawning. "I'm stiff and sore and I still feel tired. I guess I'm just weak. This ordeal has drained every ounce of strength out of me."

Morgan helped her sit up, bracing her back so she would be as comfortable as possible. She couldn't help noticing how strong he was and yet he handled her so gently. Her large smile said, *thank you*, as he handed her a big plate of breakfast with a firm suggestion that she eat heartily.

"You need to eat it all," he reminded her sternly. "We need to get your strength up so we can get you out of here."

They ate without saying anything as she was devouring her food. Morgan was pleased to see that her appetite was better. Finally he broke the silence.

"You haven't told me who you are and how you got into this mess."

Swallowing the last bite of food and taking a quick sip of coffee, she looked up at him with a satisfied smile on her face. "Well, as I told you yesterday, my name is Rose—actually Roseanna Jackson. My folks own the J bar J Ranch on the San Juan near Aztec."

"I've heard of it, " he said, nodding. "It covers a lot of territory. It's a nice spread, all right."

"I guess it is," she replied. "Dad's a strong, powerful man and does just about what he wants to, when he wants to. Right now I bet he's got half the country, including the army, out looking for me."

"What about your husband?" he interrupted.

"Husband?" There was a pause, followed by a puzzled look that turned into a slight smile. "I have no husband," she said emphatically. "Just a father, mother and two brothers. Certainly no husband!"

"I'm sorry," he apologized, then quickly added, "I mean, I'm not sorry you don't have a husband. I mean I'm sorry I got too personal with my questions."

"Please excuse me," she said, shaking her head. "I guess I'm a little sensitive about that. Please forgive me. I know my family's looking for me—I just *know* it. My poor mother," she said, choking up. "I know she's sick over all this. I wish there was a way I could let them know that I'm all right."

"I doubt if anyone will find you here," Morgan said sympathetically. "The rain pretty will eliminated any sign. This place is well hidden and hard to find. I don't know any way of letting them know, except leaving you here by yourself and I just can't do that."

"No, don't leave me alone here," she pleaded. "Please!"

"Don't worry, I won't. We'll just have to get you well as soon as possible and then take you home."

"Thank you," she said. "Thank you very much."

"Don't you ever worry about that again," he said reassuringly. "Now tell me how you got in such a mess."

"Okay," she said as she continued her story. "I was on my way to Pagosa from the ranch to see a friend and spend a few days with her. When we reached the Dyke Station, it was late afternoon. Something had broken on the stagecoach—something with the wheel. By the time they had it fixed it was late, so it was decided that we would spend the rest of the night there.

"When we arrived that afternoon, several Indians were leaving. We were told they were troublemakers and Mr. Summers had run them off. The next morning, just as we were getting ready to leave, I was standing by the stagecoach door when they came busting back into the yard shooting and hollering." Her eyes got moist as she remembered. "It was terrible!"

"Mr. Summers had run out on the porch to see what was going on and was hit by a bullet. I think he was seriously hurt and maybe dead. Then they shot one of the station hands as well as the stage driver. I saw Mrs. Summers and the two men who were passengers run out the back door and into the trees behind the station, but the Indians didn't follow them. In the meantime I ducked into the stage and lay down on the floor.

"They ransacked the station, grabbing all the whiskey they could carry. Then the tall one pulled me out of the stagecoach and threw me on his horse. They rode away from the station like the devil was after them. Leaving the road and trails, they stayed in the trees and brush. That's how I got so skinned up. After we had traveled for a few miles, they stopped and started drinking. I tried to run away but they caught me. The tall one tied my wrists together with rawhide and then tied the other end to a branch in a tree so high I couldn't reach it. Then they returned to their drinking. Thank God they were so busy gulping down the liquor that they didn't do anything else to me. After a couple more drinking stops, I guess they decided they needed to cover some ground because they rode hard without stopping anymore. After a while I got to hurting and was getting so tired. That's when everything started to go black." She stopped long enough to wipe a tear off her cheek. "I don't really remember much more. I don't even know how I got here." Reaching out and touching his hand, she added, "I'm so thankful to be here. I probably wouldn't have lasted much longer."

Morgan thought it best, anyway at the moment, not to tell her what Two Bears had planned for her future and certainly not what the rest wanted to do to her, although living all her life out here, she probably had a pretty good idea.

"I hope you didn't get hurt," she added.

"Oh, I got a little scratch, nothing serious. Believe me, I've had worse things happen to me."

Briefly he told her about the rescue. They had a laugh about the dog scaring him and the face to face encounter with the Ute. Getting up, he poured himself another cup of coffee, but she shook her head when he offered it to her. "I've had plenty," she said.

"I was sure glad to see it rain like it did," he continued as he sat down again. "I don't know if I could have handled all six of them if it had come down to a face to face fight, but thanks to that heavy rain, any sign of our whereabouts was washed away. It's probably driving them crazy trying to figure out where we are," he added with a chuckle. "By the way, Dawg here played a big part in getting you away from them and besides that he's been guarding you night and day ever since."

"Thank you...., what did you say his name was?" she asked, turning to Morgan with a puzzled look.

"I call him *Dawg*. I don't think he has any other name, not that I know of anyway."

"Well, thank you, Dawg. Thank you very much."

The man stood up, gathering up the plates and cups. He put them in the pan of hot water. "Anyway, what has happened is all water under the bridge now. The important thing is to get you up and around." He could tell she still wasn't feeling very well. "I have some warm water and there's plenty of soap if you feel up to cleaning yourself. Then you can rest some more. Maybe later today we can rig something up for you to wear."

Rose didn't need any more urging. Excusing himself, Morgan went out in the meadow to tend to the chores. When he returned, she had finished and was sound asleep. The dog was curled up at her feet, as usual. Morgan was amazed. He had never seen the animal take to anyone like he had to this woman. He hardly ever left her side. *At least*, he thought, *I don't have to worry about anyone or anything bothering her.*

He returned to his spot at the river's edge. It had returned to normal and was almost clear again. He was so deep in thought while watching the little eddies in the moving water that he hardly noticed the raising of the big trout to the surface as they devoured an occasional bug floating by. It had him puzzled, why the Utes had not returned. It just didn't figure and he couldn't get it out of his mind. He knew as well as anything that Two Bears had suspected someone was in the area. Maybe he should ride out in the morning and check things out for himself. He'd leave the dog here to look after Roseanna. A big splash interrupted his thoughts.

"Man, that old boy must have been at least two feet long," he murmured to himself. "I haven't had a nice trout supper in days. I wonder if Rose likes fish? Time I found out."

Being late in the summer, the meadow was full of big fat grasshoppers. Catching about half a dozen, he grabbed his fishing line and headed back to the pool. It took all of thirty minutes before he had four large mountain trout cleaned and ready to fry. That evening they ate without hardly saying a word. The cookfire was only glowing coals now. The sun had just started its final descent behind the low hanging clouds on the horizon. It was a beautiful sunset. The clouds were soaking up the sunshine, giving them a beautiful rosy blue hue, surrounding them with a golden halo. The crickets were providing a backround serenade as an occasional bullfrog added his contribution to the familiar noises of an evening in the mountains. Morgan broke the spell.

"Hope you like the fish. I eat a lot of them. Love catching them and I don't believe in wasting things, so I've developed a taste for them."

"They were good," she nodded as she licked her fingers. "We don't have opportunity to eat them very often at home."

"Well, we'll have to see you get your fill while you're our guest." After pausing for a moment, he continued in a more serious tone. "Rose, when you wake up in the morning, I'll be gone. As a precaution I want to check things out, make sure those hostiles aren't still around."

"Won't you be taking an awful chance?" she replied nervously. "What if they're still around? What will you do? I don't want to see you getting hurt again."

"I'll be careful and I won't take any unnecessary chances. We need to know if they went on or if they're still in the area. The dog will stay here with you, so nothing will happen to you. I won't be long and when I get back we'll have a late breakfast.

"By the way, I laid a pair of my pants and a shirt there by your bedroll. That old pair of moccasins is the only shoes I have for you to wear. You can have my knife to do any cutting you need to and I'll dig out the needle and thread I carry in my saddle bags. You'll have to excuse the needle, it's kind of large but it's been a useful tool for me. I'm sure you can make it work and that way you can fix the clothes however you need to so you can be as comfortable as possible. I know the moccasins will be too big, but maybe you can do something to make them fit you. If it will help, I'll dig up some rawhide for you to use." Rose thanked Morgan and assured him she would be fine. Lying back in her bed, she was soon fast asleep.

The eastern horizon was beginning to lighten by the time Morgan had Blue saddled and ready to go. Rose was sleeping so peacefully that he didn't have the heart to wake her. If everything went right he wouldn't be gone that long anyway, he convinced himself.

"Stay with Rose," he ordered the dog as he slipped the carbine into its scabbard and swung up into the saddle. Blue started for the opening of their camp. At the river's edge he stayed in the water, hoping it would hide his tracks. About half a mile upriver, he crossed and continued up a small creek. Leaving the creek, he reined Blue in a southwestern direction. By now it was getting light enough to see signs.

It was a beautiful morning, a gentle breeze blew softly against his face. He could feel a slight chill signaling that fall was in the air. He loved the fall of the year. There was a different feel to the air and the sounds of nature were just not the same, especially in the high mountains as the array of trees went through their change of colors. From their various shades of green in the summer, some would change to a brilliant yellow, others to rich orange and still others, like the oak brush, would be a deep red. It was pleasant to listen as one's ears picked up the music caused by the cool fall breezes rustling through the leaves and causing them to flutter softly to the ground. Adding to this, there were the little critters scurrying through the fallen leaves as they gathered food for the on-coming winter.

While doing all this daydreaming, his eyes constantly searched the ground for any signs of human presence. He had cut back to the river, following it south. There were no fresh tracks made since those last two rains. Several miles down the river, he suddenly came on some signs made after the rain. The tracks of six horses. This had to be the wayward Utes.

It was late in the afternoon when he finally returned to the camp. Rose was dressed in her new outfit.

"It wasn't too hard to get the shirt to fit," she said, as she modeled her handiwork for him. "A tuck here and there and a little sewing was all it took. The pants I just pulled together with the belt I made out of your rawhide. I redid the moccasins and they seem to fit just fine." Pausing for several moments and turning around a couple of times, she asked. "Well, what do you think?"

Morgan eyed her up and down a couple of times. This was the first time he really had had an opportunity to get a good look at the woman he had rescued. She was a beautiful, softly rounded, desirable-looking lady. She had washed and fixed her hair and it hung down her back in a single braid. He noticed for the first time just how pretty her emerald green eyes were. She had smiling eyes, big, beautiful bright eyes that complemented her dimples when she smiled. His first thought was that, at the least, Two Bears had good taste in women!

"You look great," he finally answered. "Just great!" *If she looks this good,* he thought, *in my old pants and shirt, what would she look like in a nice dress?*

"Thank you, kind sir," she said, then her smile changed to a frown. "I was starting to worry, it was getting so late. What did you find out? Are they still out there?"

"No," he replied as he started a cook fire, "no sign of them anywhere near here. Are you hungry? I'm starved!"

"Yes, I could eat a horse. But are you sure they're not around?" Worry was evident in her voice.

"Stop worrying," he assured her. "I tracked them most of the day. Apparently they went down river for several miles. The rain pretty well wiped out their tracks. When I picked up their trail again, they had turned and started to circle back, staying a mile or so from the river. They hadn't gotten far when it looked like fifteen or so riders cut their trail and started following them. They were shod horses, so I assumed it must have been a posse from Pagosa. A little ways down the trail the Utes turned and headed northwest, their pursuers right behind them." Morgan stopped for a moment and poured some coffee grounds into the boiling water. "I don't know if they caught up with them. I trailed them for awhile, but couldn't catch up with the shod horses. I decided to come back before it got any later. At least we know they're not in the immediate vicinity. I think I can guarantee that."

"I knew they would be looking for me, " she said thoughtfully.

"I wish there was a way of letting my folks know I'm all right."

"I know, but be patient and we'll get you home just as soon as you're strong enough to travel."

After eating, Rose once again laid down and spent what was left of the day sleeping. Sleep was good for her, Morgan thought. It had a way of helping the body heal itself.

****

After leaving the area of Morgan's camp, Two Bears and his confederates had returned to the large hunting camp several miles down the Piedra. His mother and grandfather were there. The renegades needed food and clothing and as the frost of fall was settling in, they would need blankets. They learned that the soldiers from Pagosa Springs had searched the village about noon that day. Not finding the renegades, they had left. About two hours later Two Bears had arrived. Afraid the posse might return, the six wanted men decided it was too risky to stay. Leaving with their supplies, they crossed the river and headed north. They should have turned northwest and hid out with one of the western Ute bands. It would have been easier to get lost somewhere between Ouray and Meeker, but Two Bears was determined to find his missing prize. Heading north, they went back to the area they had last seen her.

Coming back across the river just two miles south of where they had lost the woman, they started to make a circle, looking for signs. They hadn't gotten far when from a high ridge, they saw the soldiers coming in their general direction. It was decided that it would be best to high-tail it to the high country where they could hide until the army gave up the search. This took them in a northeasterly direction. Later that day the soldiers crossed their trail and, seeing there were six riders, decided they were most likely the ones they were after. Sending one of the civilian scouts back to Pagosa Springs for more help, they fell in behind Two Bears and his companions. That scout had met up with Brad and Larry Jackson in Pagosa and agreed to lead the brothers to the army patrol. It had rained some but the trail was still easy to follow.

The Utes had led the patrol on a merry chase. They had made it almost to the headwaters of the Piedra when they had turned due east, straight into the deep canyons and mountains of the Continental Divide. They had in mind a certain canyon where the terrain was terrible, with lots of brush and trees. Huge rocks that nature had dislodged over time were scattered everywhere. The piñons, pines and oak brush grew thick among the rocks, even hiding many little caves etched out of the surrounding canyon sides. You could be so close to someone you could hear them, but it was almost impossible to get a clear shot unless you were perched high on the surrounding mountain side that afforded a clear view of the canyon floor. Still, even then it would be hard to locate and keep track of them.

The soldiers had trailed the renegades to the mouth of this canyon. An old prospector, who had helped the army as a guide several times in the past, called it the Devil's Run. They decided to halt for a break, planning what their next move would be. They were practically out of food and water. The old prospector, a man by the name of Jeb Hardman, had a suggestion. "I knows the Devil's Run well and it's rough. Ifn' the Injuns knows it well, and I suspect they does, they'll be able to go through fast. It'll be slow for us because they could hide in there and double back on us or make it hard on us to follow, or leave fast and by the time we'uns get through, they'll be long gone. We'll never catch 'um."

The sergeant, a big, burly Irishman, shook his head. "We're going to have to turn back soon, if the men I sent for don't find us. Our food is almost gone and it won't be long before we'll have to stop and hunt for water. We might have to call it quits until we can return to Pagosa and get better organized. We've got their names and descriptions so we'll get them eventually. Trouble is, will the young lady last that long?"

Jeb, deep in thought, spoke up. "I've been doing some figuring. I'm thinking there's only one easy place to come out of the canyon on the yonder end. I'm also thinking them redskins will figure we might think theys gonna double back, so they hightail it to the other end and climb out of ol' Devil's Run and be halfway to Wyoming before we'uns figure out what's happened."

"So, what can we do, Jed?" a weary trooper piped up.

"Well, I was thinking....from the looks of their track they're just ahead of us. I knows a shortcut from here to where they'd have to come out of the canyon. One part of the trail is kinda risky—it goes close to the edge of a drop-off and there's some shale. If we lead the hosses and walk careful-like, we'll be all right. If we goes into the canyon, I know we couldn't git them. Wouldn't have a snowball's chance in hell of doing it. But if they do skedaddle, like I knows they will, we can be at the rim of the canyon waiting for them."

"What do you think, lad?" Jed asked as he cocked one eye and looked at the sergeant.

"Looks like the only chance we've got," the sergeant answered. "Let's do it." Then he added, "We'll leave about four men here just in case they double back. Now if either squad hears gunfire, come running. Come on, Jed, lead the way." Leaving four of the soldiers the sergeant trusted to stay alert, the rest started for the upper end of the canyon.

Two Bears knew this canyon well. It was about two or three miles long and about a mile at the widest part. A small stream came over the rim rock at its head and basically ran through the center. Most of the time it was dry, although this year, due to the late rains, it had some water in it. It was rimmed with rocky cliffs and in the past huge chunks of rock had come loose and rolled to the canyon bottom, literally covering most of it. With the addition of the heavy growth of trees and brush, there were a million places to hide. While a man could climb out in several places, there was only one place a horse could get out. This was at the northeast end. While the trail was pretty well hidden most of the way up, as a person topped out they were well out in the open and exposed to detection.

Two Bears had entered the canyon with the thought of losing the soldiers and then doubling back at night. His mind was still set on going back, finding the white man, and retrieving his prize. The trouble was that several of his comrades had different ideas. They wanted to get out of the canyon fast. Their plan was to head for the western side of the mountains and join their Ute brothers over on the plains of Utah. They could get lost in one of the Ute bands until this incident could blow over. This is where they made a mistake. While they stopped to argue and make up their minds as to what to do, the army had had time to get over the top and get set up and would be waiting for them to come out of the canyon. Two Bears wouldn't budge on his determination to go back and four of the others were just as adamant as to the wisdom of pressing on. Finally it was agreed that they would split up. The four would go on over the top and head west. Two Bears and Redhorse would double back and head for the Piedra River.

Brad Jackson and his party had just reached the mouth of the canyon and had been told the plans. Just then the first shots rang out, echoing down the canyon. The four waiting riders ran for their horses and decided to ride straight up the canyon bottom, staying close to the stream. They figured it was probably the quickest.

Brad hollered out, "Wait, I'm going with you!" Then turning to Larry, "You three stay here and keep a sharp eye out in case some get by the posse and decide to come out this way." With that, he started out after the soldiers.

"Joe, get the horses out of sight," Larry ordered as he dismounted. "And get up on the hillside out of sight. Make sure you can see across the canyon." Taking his rifle from the saddle boot he motioned to their guide to stay out of sight and took off to the other side. Climbing to the top of a big rock lying close to the canyon wall and lying on his belly, he was in perfect position to see across to where Joe was waiting.

Two Bears and Redhorse were working their way along the side of the canyon when the shooting started. Redhorse was in the lead as they approached the head of the canyon. Not seeing anyone, he decided to make a break for it. Before Two Bears could stop him, he urged his horse to a gallop. About this time Joe saw him and, rising up, snapped a quick shot at him. The bullet missed the Indian but caught the horse in the neck and down he went. Joe didn't see Two Bears following. The Indian raised his rifle and fired, bringing the white man down with a wound to the upper leg. About this time, Larry got a quick shot off at Two Bears, but it was short, spraying dirt on the running horse. Wheeling the black to the left, Two Bears disapppeared into the thick growth of piñon and oak brush, free of the canyon and well into the open.

Jumping down from the rock and coming to the canyon floor, Larry found the guide holding a dazed Redhorse at gunpoint. "I'll check on Joe and be right back," he yelled as he started across to where Joe was. He found Joe tying his bandana around his leg.

"Can you walk," he asked,

"Yep, I think so," Joe replied as he took a step.

"Let me help you down to the horses and we'll clean that wound and see how bad it is. One Indian got away but you brought one down. Killed his horse, but we got him and that's what counts."

There had been considerable gunfire up the canyon, but now it was quiet. After tying up the dazed Indian and putting the guide high on the hillside to keep watch on things, Larry decided to build a fire and heat some water to clean Joe's wound. The sun was just going down and it was cooling off. They'd need to fix some supper, as they hadn't eaten all day. It was just after dark when the army patrol and their captives reached the fire. One renegade had been killed, two slightly wounded, the fourth was unhurt. One trooper had been grazed by a bullet. Otherwise the rest were fine.

"Was Rose with them?" Larry asked Brad even before he could dismount.

"Nope, she wasn't," he replied as he wearily dismounted.

"Is she alive...dead?"

"I have no idea," Brad answered, shaking his head. "They told us they took her but a white man sneaked into their camp that first night and took her. They swear they don't know where she is now, or whether she's dead or alive."

"Wouldn't a white man have brought her back in by now? At least to Pagosa?" Larry asked.

"You'd think so," Brad answered. "But I got to thinking, well, you know how fragile she is. Maybe she's too weak and they're holed up somewhere until she gets stronger. I can only imagine how rough it was on her. Here's a thought—if she died, he would have brought her straight to Pagosa. I have a gut feeling that she's all right. Maybe by now...she's safe."

The wounded had been cared for. Two fires had been started, one for cooking supper and the other to keep the captives warm. They had been tied securely and given some food, which they refused. After supper Brad talked the sergeant into interrogating them once more. Although Redhorse was defiant and wouldn't answer any questions, one of the others seemed more agreeable to talk, especially after one of the interpreters hit him a good one on the jaw. He wouldn't budge from the story that a white man took her. They did find out about the determination of Two Bears to find her and kill the man who had taken her. Later Larry and Brad sat around the fire drinking coffee and discussing what they should do now.

"The soldiers are heading back to Pagosa in the morning," Brad said. "They're going to take the body of the dead Indian back. The wounded will need some attention also. We'll send Joe back with them. The sergeant is convinced Rose was not with them and if they are telling the truth, she'll show up. He said the army would get Two Bears eventually. I think the Indian may have an idea where she is. You and I will spend a few days seeing if we can track him. I would sure like to get my hands on that heathen. Jeb said he'd go with us since he knows this country like the back of his hand."

The next morning after the larger group had left for Pagosa, Larry, Brad and Jeb started out to find Two Bears. Sure enough, when they got to the head of the canyon, they found the signs of an unshod horse going out over the top and turning back towards the

Piedra River, but Two Bears was not a fool and soon they lost his trail.

"He's goin' to hole up somewheres and wait us out," was Jeb's comment.

"Well, I'm not giving up yet," Brad replied, "Let's keep circling for a few days and see what pops up. If we can't find him then we'll head back to Pagosa and hope for the best."

Five

The next couple of days went without incident. Roseanna slept most of the time and Morgan could tell she was feelling better. He spent most of the time just puttering around. He did get the horses shod and there were a few other minor details to take care of.

It was late in the morning when Rose found him out in the meadow. He was sitting on a stump by the little stream fixing a torn strap on the rigging that held the panniers on Millie's back. He was happy to see her out in the sunshine and walking fairly steadily too. Her wounds were healing well. There didn't seem to be any infection and she didn't complain about her wrists any longer. A healthy color was returning to her face and those pretty green eyes were clearing and that special sparkle was getting brighter every day. Stopping, she yawned and stretched her arms above her head.

"I feel a little better this morning" she sighed, "and thought I would get out and stretch my legs a bit." For a few minutes she looked around. "So this is your home away from home," she said, bringing her gaze back and extending her hand to him. "Well, are you going to show me around?"

"Sure, be glad to," he said with a grin. Laying the strap down and standing up, he held his hand out to her, which she promptly took. Then he slowly walked her around the meadow, showing her all the special features of his little domain. When they got back to the stump, a slight breeze had started to blow. It was a pleasant sound as it rattled the leaves in the quakies, which blended nicely with the backround noise of the river.

"You take the stump," he said. "I'll just park here on the ground."

"It's so beautiful here," she sighed as she sat down, wiping a few strands of straying hair out of her face. "So quiet and peaceful, like there's no other world out there. It's as if we are the only two people on earth."

"I know," he replied. "That's why I try to spend some time here each summer. Where this stream is running must have been the old river bed. I find a little gold here on each trip. Over by the cliff, several springs feed the stream, so there's plenty of cool, fresh water. Besides," he added, "the fishing in the river is great. What more could a man want?"

"How on earth did you find it?" she wanted to know.

"By accident, I guess you'd say."

"Accident?"

"Well, maybe necessity is a better word," he said, looking at the ground. "Actually I was trying to save my skin!"

"What does that mean?" She looked puzzled.

"It means that I was trying to find a place to hide." His face flushed a light shade of pink.

"You mean," she asked in a teasing way, "you were running from someone? This I've got to hear." A big smile covered her face.

"Well, you can chuckle all you want to, but sometimes it's better to run and hide, at least a man can keep on living that way."

"I was only teasing," she said with a mischievous gleam in her eyes. "Please go on. I really would like to hear the story."

"Are you sure?" he asked hesitantly.

"I'm sure," she answered. "I wouldn't miss it for the world!"

"Well, several years ago," Morgan began as he leaned back on one elbow and stared out towards the river, "I was working as a guard for a mining company. We would make trips in and out of the mountains, sometimes by wagon, sometimes by mule. We would take the ore from the mines high on the Continental Divide and bring it down to the smelters and then we'd take supplies back on the return trip.

"On one certain trip we were returning with a full load of supplies. For some unknown reason, old man Grubbs, the man I was working for, was having us bring a large amount of cash back to the mine. We were coming back and were following this river back up to the mine. We had just reached this spot when bandits hit us. They ambushed us from the trees and it happened so fast that we didn't even have a chance to fight back."

"Were they after the money?" she interrupted.

"That was evident since that's all they took," he replied. "How they knew about the money, we never did find out," Morgan said thoughtfully and then continued. "But before I could even get my gun out, a bullet ripped through my leg, killing my horse right out from under me. Both of us tumbled off the river bank and into the water. I had fallen free of the saddle, but my old horse sort of rolled over me as we went down. My head hit a rock and my hip got another. My leg went numb. I was dazed and had to fight to remain conscious. Lucky for me, the spring thaw was still going on and the river was still running high. Going limp, I let the current carry me down stream. I pulled myself to the other side where a large thicket of willows was growing.

"Because of the high water the willows were flooded and I pulled myself deeper and deeper into them. I don't know how it happened, but I came up out of the willows right at the narrow opening to this meadow."

"Maybe someone was helping you." She spoke thoughtfully.

"That's not likely," he hurriedly replied. "There I was laying on the ground, trying to catch my breath. I could hear the bandits finishing their slaughter of everyone. They even killed the mules. I don't know when they left because I passed out and didn't come to for several hours, sometime in the early morning. My aching head had a big knot on it and my leg was throbbing and hurting something fierce. The bad guys were gone by then. Everything was quiet on the other side of the river. I figured I better get back across as soon as I could. I had lost my pistol in the river and my rifle was still in its scabbard on my saddle. Being unarmed out here is kind of like being undressed. In fact, it's downright dangerous!

"I couldn't bear much weight on my bad leg, but I was fortunate that the same leg took both the bullet and the bruise from the river boulder." Pausing, Morgan gestured with his hands. "Would you believe, I had a bruise that big on my hip and about a foot below that was the bullet hole in the fleshy part of my leg.

"I hobbled over to this stream and washed the blood off my

head. The cool water helped clear out the cobwebs. After cleaning the wound on my leg as best I could, I tied my bandana around it to protect it. The next thing was to get back across the river. Working myself back through the willows, I reached the moving current but couldn't stand up in it. So I let the water carry me and somehow I managed to get back across. Once across, the first thing was to get a pistol off one of the dead miners since he wouldn't be needing it anymore. My dead mare was lying headfirst, about half in the water. While my saddle bags were still dry, my rifle was wet and muddy. Finally I got everything off her and up on the bank.

"I carried my things up the hillside a piece, just inside the trees. there I would be hidden and still keep my eye on the dead mules and supplies. I know Grubbs would be sending out a search party when we didn't show up at the right time. But in the meantime, I didn't know who else might come around. The buzzards were starting to circle high in the sky and that could be an invitation for all kinds of scavengers, both the four *and* two-legged kind. After getting a fire started, I warmed up some water and re-dressed my wounds and cleaned up my saddle and gun. Then after eating a bite, I spent some time covering up the dead men with some tarp from the supplies and securing their bodies so animals would leave them alone. All there was to do then was to wait. The only living things that showed up were the buzzards and some coyotes who came in at night to eat on the dead mules."

"How long did you have to wait for help to come?" she asked.

"Grubbs and three of his men showed up a couple of days later. The men stayed to bury the dead and guard what was left of the supplies until more mules could be brought in to pack them out. The old man and I went back to the mine, where I was laid up for a couple of weeks. I didn't want to leave until I could ride without a lot of pain. When I could get around fairly well, I bought myself a horse, said good-bye to Mr. Grubbs, and headed back to this place. I was hoping there would be signs to follow, but too much time had passed. When I got here I stayed a couple of days. Looking around and doing some exploring, I came to the conclusion that it was a perfect hide-away. Not only that, but I found a few pieces of gold. It occurred to me that this place afforded privacy, good shelter, plenty of food and water for my animals and a stream full of trout just for the taking. I had a good rest before I started out to trail the bandits. I figured with money they'd head for the closest town or the other side of the mountains."

"Did you find them?" Rose asked impatiently.

"No, I never did. Right away I figured the trail was too old. What was left of their tracks led me to the main road between Pagosa Springs and Animas City, but then I had no idea which direction they went or even if they stayed on the road. After two months of riding and asking questions, I came up empty-handed."

Rose interrupted. "Makes you wonder who they were to just disappear like that!"

"I have a theory," mused Morgan. "Old man Grubbs was a sorry old man and he was crooked and had short-changed a lot of folks. Yes, sir, he had made a lot of enemies. I think one of them got even, took back what he figured was owed him. You know, it wasn't six months later that someone ambushed and killed the old buzzard. Shot him in the back."

"Tell me," she said anxiously, "what did you do then?"

"Rode up around Silverton, did odd jobs for some of the bigger miners—mainly bringing in supplies for them." Morgan paused thoughtfully. "But, you know, I never forgot this place. I've returned many times since that first time...yep...*many* times."

There was silence for some minutes, each off in their own little private world. Finally Rose asked, "Fletcher, I'm curious. Just where is your home?"

"Here," he said, looking at her with a smile on his face.

"No," she replied, shaking her head. "I don't mean this place. I mean, where are you from? Where do you live when you're not in the mountains. Don't you have family and friends?"

"Well, I reckon these mountains are the only home I have or want."

"You mean you don't belong somewhere else?" she said with disbelief. "I mean, besides these mountains? Somewhere you call home—a house you live in?"

"No, I can't say that I do," Morgan said, shaking his head.

Not willing to give up, Rose continued. "Where do your father and mother live?"

"They're both dead."

"Oh, I'm sorry," Rose said sympathetically, and then tried another approach. "Okay, where were you born then?"

"Denver," Morgan said and in anticipation of her next question added, "but I did most of my growing up in Animas City. In fact, my only brother lives there. Well, that may not be exactly true. I heard he moved to Durango. Really doesn't matter, I guess, since there's only spitting distance between them anyhow." Pausing, he continued. "You see, I don't see my brother very often."

"You mean he's your only relative?"

"I have some back east, but I've never met them."

"Fletcher, I must seem nosy to you, " she said in a sincere way, "but honestly I'm not really that way. It's just that I'm curious to know more about you. If you don't want to talk about it, I'll stop asking."

"No, that's all right, I don't mind you asking. It's just that some things in my life are painful to talk about, I have to admit, though, it's been nice to have someone to talk with." In fact, it surprised him that he was even discussing these things that he had in the past always kept to himself.

Rose was puzzled as she continued. "It's hard for me to understand how lonely it must be not to have a special place where you feel you belong. Where you have put your roots down and built a life for yourself and a family. You know, the passing on of your name and a heritage to future generations....a place to call home."

Morgan paused for a moment, trying to figure out a way to explain to her how he felt. "When it comes to a home, I guess I'm a lot like the Utes."

"The Utes!" she exclaimed. "How in the world can you be like them?"

"We're alike in a lot of ways," he explained. "Did you know that once they could call home all the mountain ranges of Colorado? They even ranged out on the eastern plains, out towards Kansas, as well as a big part of the Utah Territory. During the warmer parts of the year they would live high in the mountains, hunting, fishing, taking care of their families and enjoying the beauty and serenity of God's creation. They would take long rides whenever they took a mind to. They were free to go and do what they wanted, when they wanted. In colder months, they would come down to the lower elevations and spend the winter. The mountains provided them with all they needed—food, clothing, shelter and what they couldn't find in the mountains, they'd take from their neighbors.

"It's sad, because gradually most of their land that they called home was taken from them. First they were moved back off the plains and confined to the mountains. Then the miners came for the gold and silver, so they were told to leave the mining areas and now they have been confined to small reservations. Their natural home and the freedom it offered have been very limited."

"You actually feel sorry for them, don't you?" Rose said.

"Yes, I do," Morgan replied sharply. "I've been living the same way for the past few years—during the summer months roaming here and there through the higher mountains. During the winter I hole up somewhere in the lower foothills where the snow isn't so deep. I know how I would feel if someone forced me out of this way of life."

"Well, after what they did to me," she said empathically, "I don't feel sorry for them! I hate them!"

"Rose, let me tell you a truth. You don't throw the bucket of apples away just because there's one bad one in it. If there's one thing I've learned for sure in my traveling around the country, it's that whether a person is good or bad has nothing to do with their color, race, age, education, or culture. You just can't judge the whole by what a few do. Just because a few Indians were bad and hurt you doesn't make all Indians bad. I've seen good and bad Mexicans, good and bad white folks, there's good and bad in all different cultures. I guess what it boils down to is this—whoever has the biggest gun is the one who gets to say what is right and wrong or what color of a man's skin is better. At this point in history, it's the white man who calls the shots. I try to judge a man by what he does and what he says, not by who he is. Their eyes can tell you a lot about them."

"Wait! I didn't want to start an argument," she said in an apologetic way, "but it's hard for me to feel any different right now."

"I understand that and I can't say I blame you. I don't cotton to many of the things the Utes do. Stealing and hurting others because of some customs they have. I certainly don't condone what they did to you. From our standards it's wrong. But try to look at it from their point of view. Their culture is far different from ours. It is as if they and the land were one...they are a part of it, belonging to it...not like the white man who feels he must own the land and exclude others from using it. In their culture and before the white man came, it was an honorable thing for them to raid their enemies. They would take horses, people, food, or whatever they needed. They did not regard it as stealing when they took what was their enemy's and they would fight to the death to protect what was theirs. When the white man came, they were generally willing to share, but instead they were gradually pushed out of their ancestral lands onto reservations. I imagine that there is a little bit of bitterness and many may resent what has happened. It's human nature to fight back. Take you, for example, do you know why they took you?"

"No, not exactly, but I can guess," she said, "and it's not good."

"Well, let me tell you what I gathered by what little I heard. It seems that the tall one, I think his name is Two Bears if I translated right, apparently was fascinated by the color of your eyes and hair, so much so, that he decided to take you for his woman."

"He what?" she yelled in disbelief. "You can't be serious!"

"I'm afraid so," he assured her. "You almost got married. How does Mrs. Two Bears sound?" he asked, not able to hold back a chuckle.

"It's not a laughing matter," she replied, as she fought back the urge to join in the laughter.

"Why I decided to tell you," he said, "is because I don't think Two Bears meant to harm you. He probably didn't realize you couldn't take the harsh treatment. Now the others are a different story. They were upset with Two Bears for taking you. They figured it was going to cause them a lot of trouble, which is probably true. They may have ended up hurting you."

"You may have a point," she admitted. "I mean about not blaming all Utes because a few hurt me. I'll have to think about it. It's kind of funny, though, isn't it? I mean, him wanting me for a wife....but I don't want to think about it anymore. Let's change the subject and talk about you again. What on earth do you do all winter? If you don't have a home to go to, where do you stay?"

"Well, one winter I spent at Fort Lewis, working for the Army. Let's see, the next one I spent most of the time healing from a pretty nasty wound. Laid around Sally's Boarding House in Durango. The last two, I've stayed on a little ranch up the Florida. It belongs to an older couple. I did odd jobs for them, you know, like mending fences and other things they needed done."

"You worked on a ranch?" she exclaimed, a look of surprise written all over her face.

"Yes, as a matter of fact, I did," he retorted. "You know, I haven't anything against work. The truth is I enjoy working when it accomplishes something good."

"I'm sorry," she apologized, "I didn't mean to hurt your feelings. It just surprised me, that's all. Now tell me, how on earth did you run into a deal like that?"

"First of all, you didn't hurt my feelings and to prove it, I'll tell you. It started when I was scouting for the Army. The only real friend I had at the Fort was a kid by the name of George Olsen. His folks are the ones that own this ranch. He would go home and visit them now and then and sometimes I would go along. They took a liking to me and, well, I felt real comfortable around them. They tried to teach me a little about ranching and I enjoyed being able to help them out. I guess it was just about three years ago that George was killed in some trouble with the Utes up north. When I heard about it, I went to see his parents to tell them how sorry I was. They not only lost a son but I lost a good friend. They invited me to come see them anytime and stay as long as I wanted to. So I have spent the last two winters helping them out and it's provided a nice, warm place for me to stay."

"Are they all alone?" was her next question.

"No, Mr. Olsen hired a Mexican family to stay with them and help him and Mrs.Olsen, but it's still a lot for the two of them. They're getting along in years, and I think they were holding on so George would have a place to go after he got the Army out of his system. The family he hired, the Garcias, have three sons and they do most of the work now."

"What will they do?" Rose asked.

"Last winter they were talking about selling and moving to town," he replied. "I guess time will tell."

Rose sat silent for several minutes, staring off into space, caught up in her thoughts of Morgan's conversation. Coming back from her dream world and looking up at the sky, she spoke again. "It's going to be a beautiful evening. The air is so still I can hear the water running in the river and it's a wonderful sound. By the way, what river is it?"

"It's the Piedra."

"It's a beautiful river," she said. "I can understand why you enjoy it." She paused and stood up. "I'm getting very tired so I think I'll go lay down for awhile."

"Okay," he replied, "I'll cook us some supper after while."

He watched her walk back to the campsite. She was right. It *was* a beautiful river and he *did* enjoy it. He had been from one end of it to the other, from its headwaters to where it empties into the San Juan River. Starting up on the western slope of the Divide, the Piedra ran southward until it emptied into the San Juan at the Colorado-New Mexico border. Of the six rivers in the area, this river probably was Morgan's favorite. He had explored every foot that was possible to get to. There were sections where the water passed through deep rocky canyons which neither man nor beast could travel. At times, sitting on his horse high on the mountain side, looking down at the river so far below in the rugged canyon, he wished he could see these areas, but had never taken the time or the risks in doing so. This stream had offered him many hours of pleasure, fishing and panning for gold. Just a few miles south of where Williams joined the Piedra, Sand Creek met and added its water to the river. It was in this area that Morgan had stumbled on his favorite camp and it was here at this camp that he had crossed paths with Roseanna Jackson.

Six

Later that evening after another supper of fried trout, Rose was sitting on her bedroll. Morgan was sitting on the ground cross-legged savoring a cup of hot coffee. Her gaze was fixed on the six-foot-two man who had rescued her. Curiosity was getting the better of her. What kind of man was he? He was well built, a strong physical specimen of a man. His hair was dark brown and his eyes were a light hazel that had a soft, gentle look. Although he didn't smile much and generally had a sober expression on his face, she knew he was a kind man, just from the way he treated her and the animals in his care. It was evident that he was an educated person, but why was he out here in the wilderness?

The sun had gone down by now and the air had a slight chill to it. Morgan put a couple of logs on the fire. As they ignited, the flames started casting eerie shadows on the wall of their shelter.

Rose sat silently watching him and waiting for him to settle down. Sitting back down on the ground and leaning back on his saddle, he finished the last bit of coffee left in his cup. Rose took the opportunity to speak up.

"Fletcher," she asked, "why did you choose this kind of life?"

The question caught him off guard and for a moment he just sat there thinking about it. "Circumstances, I guess," he replied thoughtfully as he stared at the ground.

After a long pause, she asked softly, "Are you going to tell me about these circumstances?"

"Oh...I'm sorry," he said as he looked up from staring at the ground and fixed his gaze on her. "I kind of got lost in my thoughts. I reckon in a man's life when he comes to a fork in the road, he has to choose one or the other. Either he takes the one to the left or he takes the one to the right. Then he has to follow it to see where it leads. If he's lucky and he's made a good choice, everything will be great."

"But," she asked, "what if you take the wrong fork? Can't you get off that road anytime you choose or even backtrack and try the other one?"

Morgan thought for a moment. "Yep, I reckon you can if you wanted to badly enough, if you really don't like the direction you're traveling or where you'll likely end up. But on the other hand, sometimes when you start down that road, there's no stopping or backing up. It's just easier to keep traveling straight ahead and go where the path takes you. Maybe I can explain it to you this way. Sometimes when you're dealt a hand of cards, something compels you to play them out, win or lose. I guess that's the way it was with me. I had to play out the hand dealt me in this game of life."

"What was your fork in the road, Fletcher?"

There was a long pause. He didn't know if he wanted to talk about it. Rose, seeing the expression on his face through the flickering fire light, sensed his hesitation.

"If you'd rather not talk about it, it's all right," she assured him.

Getting up, he poured himself another cup of coffee. Walking to the front of the shelter, he stared off into the darkness for some minutes. He took a sip of coffee as he turned and faced her. "I've never really talked to anyone about this before."

"You can tell me. I'm a good listener and I won't tell a soul."

Somehow Morgan believed her and he felt comfortable talking with her. "Well," he said, "my fork in the road was the choice I made when my mother and father were killed. If that had not happened, I'm sure my life would have taken a very different trail."

Morgan's mind went back to that July day, eleven years ago. He would never forget it if he lived to be a thousand. It was etched in his brain like a brand on a steer. Generally he had been successful in not thinking about it, just blocking it out of his mind. He wondered if he could ever face the reality that those bad years were gone.

"What on earth happened to them?" she asked.

"They were murdered in cold blood!"

"Murdered? Are you serious...who'd do a thing like that?"

"Scum, that's who."

Waiting patiently, she gave him time to continue. Finally he began.

"Dad was the town's blacksmith. His business was booming. With the influx of miners and farmers into the area, there was more work than he and I could do, so he hired another man to help out. This meant he would need more equipment and iron supplies. So he got a couple of wagons and hired two more men to help him go to Santa Fe and pick up the needed things. My mother wanted to go because she needed things, too, but Dad said *no*. He told her it wasn't safe for her to go. So they argued about it until he gave in, like he always did, and agreed that she could go along.

"They left early one morning, headed south along the Animas River. They had only gotten about fifteen miles when they were stopped by four men with intentions of robbing them. Evidently they had gotten wind of the cash Dad was carrying. This all happened where the road comes off the mesa winding its way down the steep hillside to the river below. It's a rugged hill, covered with big boulders and scrub trees. It's almost straight down. My folks were in the lead wagon and the other wagon was right behind them. They were just at the top of the descent when all of a sudden these four riders came out of the piñon trees and ordered the wagon to halt.

"The man in the second wagon instinctively went for his six-gun, but he didn't even get a shot off before he and the driver were shot down. At the burst of gunfire, the team Dad was driving bolted and started down the hill at a full gallop. The bandits took off after them, blazing away. On the first curve, the front wheel of the wagon must have hit a rock or something, causing the wagon to swerve off the road. It rolled clear to the bottom of the rocky hillside. There wasn't much left of it *or* my folks. After robbing all the bodies, the bandits headed south.

"The other driver, who had been shot, wasn't hurt that bad. He had pretended to be dead and as soon as the four men left, he caught one of the horses and rode back to town to get help. By the time we got back to the scene there were only a couple of hours of daylight left." Pausing, Morgan had to compose himself. In a few minutes he continued. "I'll never forget the feeling of anger and frustration that I felt when we reached that hillside. We found Mom about a quarter of the way down, her body broken in a dozen places. The wagon must have rolled over her. Dad was a little farther down the hill, the rocks and brush had beaten him into a bloody pulp. I felt so helpless standing and looking at them. Just that morning they were so full of life, laughing and joking with each other and going over and over the instructions to Taylor and me, on what to do and what not to do while they were gone. Now they were just lying there, still, the life snuffed right out of them. I felt like I was going to blow up because of the pressure inside me. I desperately wanted to let out a scream, but I couldn't make a sound. A good friend of the family took Taylor and me back up to the top of the hill while the others gathered up the folks. We put them and the other fellow in a wagon and headed back to town. It was almost morning before we got back to the house with them."

Rose sensed that he was still hurting and she suspected that eleven years had not completely healed the wound he had suffered by his parents' death. It was dark now, so she could not see his face clearly, but she didn't have to. She could hear the anger in his voice.

"I'm so sorry," she said sympathetically. "I don't know what I would do if I lost my parents like that. I don't know how on earth you've coped with it. Did they catch the killers?"

"Yes, but not for a long time. The next day a posse went looking for them but they couldn't find a trace, just some tracks headed south. They had left the country. Everyone figured they were heading to Mexico. The marshal notified the authorities, but came up empty-handed. Later, after all the arrangements for the funeral had been made, I looked up the wounded driver. We went over all the details he could remember of the day before. I especially wanted their descriptions and I asked him to remember everything he could about the four men. Those descriptions I burned deep into my memory."

Morgan paused for a few minutes, deep in thought. He could still remember every detail of what they looked like. Of course the driver didn't know their names, but he gave Morgan a fairly accurate description of them. He said he had seen a couple of them hanging around town the last few days. He described the four outlaws as two white men in their middle thirties, an older white man and a Mexican. It was the two younger white men he had seen in town. With their descriptions, in time Morgan put a name to each one of them.

Matt Bell was their self-appointed leader. He was a tall husky man. He had a gaunt, sneering face with long brown hair and dark eyes that were shifty and piercing. He generally wore a short beard to hide a long scar on his left jaw that went down and across his neck. He had a cutting tone in his voice that sent a message to people that he meant business. People generally left him alone. His disposition wasn't any better than his looks and he had a mean streak that wouldn't quit. Despite his rotten personality, he had a good mind and a knack of figuring ways of making a living without working very hard and at someone else's expense.

Bob Bell, Matt's cousin and two years his junior, was shorter and heavier-set than Matt. He had a full round face with brown hair and eyes to match and was generally clean-shaven. He was mentally slow and had a hard time thinking for himself, so he did very little decision making, looking to his cousin for direction. He also stuttered and that wasn't helped by his high, squeaky, irritating voice. What made him especially dangerous was his devotion to

Matt. Matt took care of all his needs, protected him and made sure nobody made fun of his stuttering. In turn, Bob would do anything Matt asked him to do, whether it was to steal, lie or even kill. Matt, therefore, always had someone to watch his back.

The Mexican was also a dangerous one. Though he didn't necessarily look like a cold-blooded killer, he was. He carried a concealed knife, as well as a small gun, inside his shirt. He enjoyed cutting a man up and leaving him to die. He was of a lean, muscular build with a handsome baby-like face. He had a full head of jet black hair and eyes as dark as the night. He was always smiling with both his mouth and eyes. He wore dark clothes that were kept clean and neat. He kept his hair neatly trimmed and had a polite, musical voice. He fancied himself a ladies man, which led to many a fight and many times ended in bloodshed. He also liked to leave the thinking to Matt.

The fourth member of the gang didn't seem to fit. He was an older man with steel blue eyes, a weathered face and graying beard and hair. He was a thin, wiry sort of fellow with a course, raspy voice. His hat drooped down around his ears and neck and he wore a pair of old bib overalls. Morgan never did know his real name, although some thought it to be *Sawyer*. Everyone just called him *the old man.* One thing was for sure, he was not to be trusted. He carried a shotgun and was a back shooter as well as an outright liar. He found it easier to follow along with Matt Bell than have to worry about taking care of himself.

This group had been together for several years, roaming around the southwest, taking what they needed from law-abiding people, not staying in one place long enough to be brought to justice. Finally Rose broke the silence.

"I'll bet I know what you did!" she stated. "You started hunting them down, didn't you?"

"You got that right. As we were all standing there in the graveyard watching Mom and Dad's caskets being lowered into that cold ground, I made a vow. I promised them that I wouldn't rest until their murderers had paid the supreme penalty for their crimes.

"After the funeral services, Taylor and I talked things over. You know, what we were going to do with the things that had belonged to our parents—the business, house, and property. He was positive that he didn't want to be a blacksmith. Since he had been working part-time down at the General Store, Mr. Higgins offered him the extra room above the store. It would give him a place to live. So he decided that's what he wanted to do—continue learning the store-keeping trade. Taylor liked that kind of work. He had always been good with numbers and got along well with people. People seemed to like him and he liked to be around them. He was one of those guys who never met a stranger.

"I made it clear that I didn't want to be a blacksmith either, that I had another job to do before I could decide what to do with the rest of my life. *Don't go after them,* he told me. *You'll only get hurt, and what good will that do?* But my mind was made up. So we decided to take an offer that had been made on Dad's business. Our home was on the same piece of property so it went with the sale. Some of their personal things we decided to keep and we stored them in a shed out back with some of our other things. The rest of their things we just left in the two buildings and walked away. The next day I bought me a good horse, a pistol, a rifle, lots of bullets and enough supplies to get me started on the trail. Said my good-byes in Animas City and rode out. I went a fair piece out in the woods and set me up a camp. Spent days practicing with the guns until I could handle them fairly well. Got up one morning, said *so long* to my mountains and headed south."

"Did you catch them?" Rose asked anxiously.

"Well, yes and no!" Morgan replied with a chuckle. "For two years I trailed them all over the southwest territories—Arizona, New Mexico and Texas, always just a step behind. They didn't stay very long in any one place and it seemed like they didn't hit too many places twice. About a year after the folks' death, one of them, the Mexican, was killed around Waco, Texas. Someone put a knife in his back. They had buried him the day before I got there and the others had already high-tailed it back to New Mexico. I chased those three for another year and finally tracked them to the Las Cruces area. When I got there, I learned they were in jail in El Paso, waiting to be hanged. A posse had rounded them up after a fouled-up bank robbery.

"When I got to El Paso and explained to the sheriff the circumstances of my being there, he let me see them. I confronted them, letting them know what my intentions had been. It didn't faze them a bit. They just laughed when I told them that when I caught up with them I had planned to gun them down in the street like mad dogs. I spit at them and walked away. I hung around and watched them swing. It wasn't a pretty sight. It makes a man sick to his stomach to witness a thing like that."

"Did watching them die give you peace of mind?" Rose asked in a soft voice.

"In a way. A huge load was taken off my shoulders and my vow had been fulfilled, but the hurt and emptiness were still there."

Pausing and reflecting on the experience, Morgan finally added quietly, "Rose, I learned something about revenge that day they swung by their rotten necks! It's not near as sweet as you think it's going to be. Oh, I felt justice had been served, but it didn't make things return to the way they were before. It didn't bring my father and mother back. All those things I loved were still gone, and the anger and frustration, because of my helplessness to make things right, were still with me.

"All the way back to the mountains I kept thinking that I had wasted two years of my life and for what? I had chased them for all that time and hadn't even laid a hand on them. In fact, I didn't even play a part in bringing them to justice! If I had never left Animas City, justice would still have been served. Besides that, on the way home I had time to think about the kind of person that I had become. I was cranky and short-tempered, caring little for the feelings of others. I would fight at the drop of a hat, though I'll admit I didn't try to start any ruckus. At the same time, I wouldn't back down or step out of the way. I shot several men and the only good thing about that was that nobody died. I got good with my six-gun and wouldn't hesitate for a second about using it. I had become a stranger to myself and didn't like what I saw in the mirror."

"Has your thinking changed now?" Rose interjected. "I mean, would you do things differently, if you could?"

"If you're asking if I would still go after them, yes I would. It would be something I'd have to do. But I've done a lot of thinking these past few years roaming around these mountains. If I had it to do over again I wouldn't let the hate and bitterness possess and eat at me as I did then. I would accept what happened as a part of life. You may not like what happens, but sometimes that's all you can do about it. You just learn to live with it."

Without realizing it, they had talked for several hours. The fire was just a few glowing embers now.

"It's pretty late," Morgan said. "I reckon it's time to turn in."

"I know," she said, "but first tell me what you did when you got back here."

"Well, like I said, I had gotten where I was pretty handy with my six-gun and, being fairly strong, I could handle myself in a fight with the best and with the rotten attitude I had at that time, I didn't hesitate to use either. Anyway, when I got back, I stopped in Taylor's store for a visit. He introduced me to one of the mine operators and he offered me a job riding guard for the mule trains that went in and out from his mine up in the La Plata. It was easy money and I liked being out in the open, so for three years I did that. When I could, I spent some time at Fort Lewis. The army had moved Fort Lewis from Pagosa Springs in the early 1880s to a spot on the La Plata River a few miles south of Parrott City. The La Plata mountains played an important part in the development of the area. La Plata means *silver* in Spanish and the newly-formed county took on that name. Parrott City was made the county seat. When the silver started to die out, Parrott City slowly died too, so the county seat was moved to Durango." Morgan cleared his throat and continued. "The Army offered me work as a scout, being's I knew the area like the back of my hand. I lasted a couple of years doing that, but I just didn't fit in with that kind of life. So I said good-bye to them and for the last four years or so, I have just wandered around in the mountains, panning for gold here and there, fishing the streams and in general just enjoying the great outdoors." He paused again. "I think I've talked enough for one night. It's time to hit the sack."

"But I have other questions," she said, not wanting him to quit talking.

"They can wait. Tomorrow's another day. Good night, Rose."

"Okay," she agreed reluctantly, as she snuggled down in her bedroll, "but you will tell me more tomorrow, promise?"

"I promise. Sleep tight."

Seven

Rose was a lazy bones the next day. In fact, it was just past noon when she finally got up and went down to the stream to wash, doing the things ladies do when getting ready for another day. Morgan had spent all morning finishing up the repairs needed on Millie's packs. They had been needing some attention for quite a while and he didn't want them to give him any trouble on the way home. With that chore done he decided to fish for dinner. When Rose was finally ready to eat there were three nice trout almost cooked.

They ate in silence. She was absorbed in separating the bones from the flesh of the fish. Finally, with her eyes still focused on her plate, she asked him, "Is Fletcher your real name?" Looking up at him she continued, "I mean, is it your birth name?"

"Yes it is. But why are you asking me that?" he answered as he scraped his bones off his plate into the fire.

"Oh, just curious, I guess. I've never heard of anyone named Fletcher and your brother's name...Taylor. I've heard of them as last names, but never as first names."

"My mother named us both," Morgan answered as he poured himself another cup of coffee. "She always said that it was important for a person to have the right name. One that would catch people's attention, one that had a nice ring to it. One that would inspire confidence and demand respect."

"Sounds like a smart lady," Rose said, as she motioned for Morgan to pour her a cup too.

Filling her cup, he continued, "You would need to know her to understand some of the things she did. She was a very proper lady. Highly intelligent with a good education, she read everything she could get her hands on."

"Was she an outgoing person?" Rose interrupted.

"Sometimes too much," he replied. "Sometimes she would run my Dad crazy with all the activities she got involved in. for example, if there wasn't a school, she'd round up all the kids in town and teach them. They would come to the house for a few hours a day and she would instruct them in the basic things she thought they needed to have a better life. She saw to it that Taylor and I were educated to the best of her abilities. She had big plans for us. We were to be sent back east to some of the *finer schools*, as she put it, so we could become somebody important. She didn't want us to have to struggle through life as a smithy, miner, or farmer.

"Anyway, getting back to our names, she once told me she had taken my name from a book she had read. She liked it and thought it went well with Morgan, so I was named Fletcher. I don't recall her ever saying where she came up with Taylor's name."

"I wish I could have known her," Rose said wistfully. "I know I would have liked her."

"I would have liked that," Morgan replied, "the two of you knowing one another. She would have loved you."

"You know," she said, "I *would* know her if you would tell me everything you know about her."

"Like what?" Morgan asked.

"Well, things like what she looked like, what she liked to do, where she liked to go, everything you can remember."

"I wouldn't know where to begin."

"Well, for starters, what did she look like?"

"Okay, let me see. She was a very beautiful person both inside and outside. She was about five-foot-eleven, slender build and very lady-like in appearance. You would have loved her long brown hair. She wore it up in a bun whenever she was out in public, but at home in the evenings she would let it down. It was beautiful. Like I said, she was well-educated and well-mannered and very proper. Everything had to be just so. Dad would kid her about being a little nosy at times and sometimes a bit on the pushy side. I guess she spoke her mind when she felt it was important."

"Was she a church-going person?" Rose asked, trying to keep Morgan talking.

"Yes, I guess you could say she was. There wasn't a regular church building yet, but a few of the woman and a man or two met in different homes on Sundays to have their services. Taylor would always go with her—he liked going as well a she did."

"What about you and your father?"

"Mom would drag me with her once in a while, but Dad...no, he never went. He had different views toward religion. When he and I were out in the mountains, hunting or fishing or just riding, he used to say that the great outdoors was his church. He felt close to God when he was there."

"Sounds to me like Taylor favored your mother and you were more like your father."

"I suppose that's true. I liked my Dad and felt comfortable around him...liked the things he liked. And you're right, Taylor was a lot like my mother. He didn't like to go out in the woods and spend time hunting or fishing like I did. Taylor liked people like my mother did. He wanted to be more of a businessman. Remember I told you about Mr. Higgins taking him in when the folks were killed? Well, he not only married the old man's daughter, but he bought his store as well. He worked hard and no one has a better store down in Animas City and Durango. But that's enough talk for now. We can continue later," Morgan said, then added a suggestion. "You need to get out and get some exercise and get that body ready for the ride home."

Rose agreed and, taking the dog, she headed out into the meadow. She strolled here and there, stopping to visit the horses and then sitting on the old stump, dangling her feet in the cool water of the small stream. Once Morgan saw her sitting on a grassy knoll in the shade of a big old cottonwood tree talking to the dog. Later, after a late meal, Morgan got her talking about her family. Leaning back, he listened while she filled him in on her father and mother, her two brothers and life in general on the J bar J. It was late by the time they had settled down for the night. Morgan, laying in his bedroll, was still awake re-thinking the events of the day. Rose had gone to sleep quickly and he could hear her soft breathing. It was a clear night, the stars were shining brightly and it was so still, as if there wasn't any air moving at all. The only noise was the water moving across the rocks in the river bed. Even the croaking of the frogs in the willows had died down so in the stillness of his little world, Morgan lay there alone with his thoughts.

The conversations of the last few days were still running through his mind. They brought back a lot of memories that seemed so long ago....memories of his father and mother and the home they had made for him and Taylor. He couldn't help thinking about the peace and security of a good home, that one can so easily take for granted. Here one day, gone the next. In his mind he could see his parents—it was so clear—as if they were still here and alive.

His father had been a large, six-foot-three man weighing in the neighborhood of two hundred and eighty pounds. He was solid and muscular in build with massive arms, the result of being a smithy all his adult life. His round, clean-shaven face sat on a short, thick neck. His curly short hair was thinning and receding more and more with each passing year. His light, sky-blue eyes had a gentle look to them and it seemed there was always a smile on his face. He was constantly humming some tune or another in his low bass voice and it was apparent he was contented with his lot in life.

He seemed an odd match for his wife, Mary. She embraced all the qualities of a well-bred lady. Being of slight build and tall, by a woman's standards, she held her body straight and all her movements were made with a graceful air. Her beautiful face, with its fine features, sat on a long, slender neck. Her eyes were a shade lighter than the dark brown hair that hung below her shoulder blades and when she spoke, her accent was evident. Though she gave the appearance of being a delicate creature, in truth she was a very strong and dominant individual. They were different in so many ways, but in the end, these differences made their union a strong one. They had many things in common, too, and these gave their life a common purpose, so in reality theirs was a good match.

Morgan had to chuckle as he lay there thinking about their differences and how opposite their personalities were. His dad was a shy, reserved person. He liked the quiet and peacefulness of being by himself. He avoided crowds and hated to go to gatherings or get involved with community projects. On the other hand, his mother was an outgoing person, always being involved with the neighbors, loving to be around people. Clay used to kid her about having her pretty little nose in everyone's business.

Maybe it was just because they came from such different backrounds. She was originally from the eastern part of the country and, being from one of the finer families, she was well-educated and had mastered the finer things of life. He, on the other hand, was from a poor family in Denver. With limited education, he had to work like a man from a very early age. As a result, he liked to work with his hands, but she liked to use her mind in accomplishing the most good. While Clay was patient and easygoing, she wanted it done *now* and tended to ramrod things along. *Yes, they had differences,* Fletcher thought, but the things they held in common were the things that made them strong. The foremost was the love they shared. They had loved one another from the first day they met back in Denver. She had moved there to fill in as a schoolteacher. They met when he had taken his little sister to the school house to enroll her. Their love had helped them make it through the years. They learned to use their individual strengths to support the other's weaknesses. They both had enormous energy and used it to the full in living life. They loved life and all the things it afforded them. Their goal was to have a long successful life together and give their sons the best start in life they could.

A couple of times every winter, they would go out in the snow and have a winter outing. Shoveling out a big spot and building a big fire, they would warm up a pot of stew and a pot of coffee. While eating they would talk and afterwards there was playing in the snow. Probably the favorite times to Morgan was when he and his father would ride back in the mountains to the little trout streams and spend a day or two fishing. Sometimes they would fish all day side by side and hardly talk at all. Then there were those times they would sit for hours on a rock or log and listen to the mountain sounds and talk about life or whatever else came to their minds. He also remembered all the hours he would work with his father in the blacksmith shop. His father was a true artist and he taught Fletcher a great deal about taking pride in one's work and being responsible for one's obligations in life. At the same time, Taylor liked to read and study so he spent a lot of time with his mother and she taught him those same lessons of life.

It was almost dawn before he finally drifted off in sleep. It was midmorning before he rolled out of the sack and went about the day's business. As he sat drinking his morning coffee, he was thinking that it had been almost two weeks since he had taken Rose away from the Utes. She would be ready to go home soon. He figured it was time to start getting her ready for that ride.

That afternoon he saddled Blue and had Rose ride him around the meadow. She needed to get toughened up and Blue needed the exercise. They spent a few days doing this. In the evenings they would talk about their lives and families until they both knew about everything there was to know about each other. Morgan knew it would be time to leave soon. Rose was feeling better and she was regaining more strength each day. He decided that tomorrow he would start making the needed preparations for the trip. That night, during their meal, he told Rose of his plans. The next day they would take the horses out of the enclosure and hunt for a small deer. They needed to get some meat ready for the trail.

"We'll leave shortly after breakfast," Morgan told her. "I'll take the coffee pot with us and something to eat for dinner. We'll make a day of riding and see if you're ready to go home."

The next morning Morgan saddled Blue for Rose. He would ride Millie bareback. She wasn't the easiest horse to ride, but they would need her to pack the deer back to camp. After strapping his six-gun on, he made sure the rifle was loaded and ready to go. Helping Rose up on Blue and swinging his leg up over the back of Millie, they moved out of the meadow, through the willows and started up the river's edge, crossing at a point where they could go up the little stream for a while before heading back into the woods.

Until noon he showed her several scenic features he especially enjoyed. A couple where you could see for miles and the view was spectacular. They had seen several herds of deer and one of elk but he wanted to get the meat in the afternoon, on the way back to camp. They stopped on one of those beautiful places where a person could see for what seemed forever and had a bite to eat and, of course, Morgan wasn't happy until he had had a cup or two of coffee.

"Are you sore yet?" he asked her, winking at the dog.

"A little," she replied, "but nothing that would stop me."

"We'll rest for a bit and then we'll start for home. It shouldn't take long to find a deer and dress it out. We'll be home late this afternoon and then I'll cook you up the best venison steak you ever sank your teeth into."

They had only gone about a mile when they stopped at the edge of a small clearing. Sitting there for a few minutes, Morgan's eye caught the movement of a small buck coming out of the trees on the opposite side. It stopped by a big pine tree that was laying on the ground.

"Rose," he whispered, "hand me the rifle and be very quiet."

"What do you see?" she asked as she handed him the gun.

"See him, over there across the meadow by that big log?" Morgan said as he drew a bead on the deer. The report of the gunshot echoed through the mountains as the buck fell to the ground on the spot.

"Good shot!" she exclaimed.

"Yep," he said, "but if there's anyone in the area, they'll sure know about us now!"

"Riding over to where the deer lay, they tied the horses to some limbs on the fallen tree. Leaning the rifle up against the log and taking his knife out of its sheath, he started to skin the buck. In just a little while, he had it ready to go back to camp where he would finish dressing it out.

****

Two Bears had waited his pursuers out. Leaving his hiding place on the upper Piedra, he had started back to the general area of where he had last seen the pretty white woman. He was slowly working his way up a gentle hillside when he heard the echo of a rifle shot vibrating through the canyons.

Rose had been sitting on the log petting the dog, watching Morgan gut the deer. Suddenly the boom of a rifle shot shattered the stillness of the afternoon. The bullet barely missed Morgan's head as he knelt by the deer cleaning his knife off in the grass. It slammed into the log, inches from where Rose sat.

"Get behind the log!" he shouted as he hit the ground.

Rose fell backwards, tumbling to the back side of the log, the dog close by her side. Morgan reached for his rifle just as another bullet kicked dirt all over him. Standing up, he dove over the log, kicking a shell into the chamber of the rifle as he came up on his knees. Peeking over the top of the log, Morgan couldn't believe his eyes. Sitting on the black horse, just at the edge of the meadow, was the tall Ute that had shot him the night of Rose's rescue.

Two Bears sat there for a few minutes looking at them, shaking his rifle in defiance of his white enemy. Then he eased the black into the trees and Morgan saw him dismount and get behind a tree.

"Who is it?" Rose asked, still hugging the ground, afraid to get up.

"It's your friend, the big tall Indian," Morgan replied. "He finally came back. I only see *him*, though. I wonder where the rest of them are?"

"Maybe they're hiding," she said, raising up enough to barely peep over the log.

"I don't think so. They'd be wanting to show off their strength, so something must have happened to them. If that's true, we only have to contend with the one. I wonder if he still wants you for a wife or if he's just trying for revenge."

"Well, I don't know, " Rose said empathatically, "but he's not getting me, that's for sure!"

"Don't worry," he assured her, "we'll get out of this thing. Just give me a minute to think."

Pausing for a moment, deep in thought, Morgan muttered, "He's waiting us out. He missed that shot deliberately because he wants me to know who's going to kill me. He also knows we can't get to the horses without exposing ourselves to him. Probably figures he won't miss the next time. We've got to get out of here before dark. Guess we'd better take the fight to him."

Morgan quickly outlined his plan to Rose. "Can you shoot a six-gun?" he asked her as he slipped his out of its holster.

"Yes," she replied. "My brothers used to let me target practice with theirs."

"Can you reload one?"

"I think so. I've done it before."

Taking six bullets out of his gun belt, he handed them and the gun to her. "Here's what we're going to do. While you keep him pinned down for a few seconds, the dog and I are going to try and get to the trees behind us. Then I'm going to send Dawg after the Ute while I try to get in position to get a clean shot at him. I'll stay where I can watch you. I don't want anything to happen to you now.

"Now, Rose, peek over and see if you can see him. He's laying on the ground next to that big pine tree just behind a little bush."

Raising up and looking, Rose responded, "I see him, but isn't he too well hidden to hit?"

"Yes, I think so," Morgan replied, "but what I want you to do is keep him from firing for a few moments. So put the gun barrel on the log and hold it steady and then all you need to do is fire four shots at the bush. While he's ducking, I'm going for the trees, okay?"

"Okay, I have it," she replied nervously.

"Good," Mrgan said. "Then I want you to carefully reload so that if he comes at you, you can defend yourself. I'll watch from the trees to protect you while you're doing that. Any questions?"

"No, I understand," she said, shaking, "but I am frightened."

"So am I," he admitted, touching her hand, hoping to reassure her that everything was going to be all right. "Now I'm going to fire one round at him, then you fire four shots, then reload. Ready?"

"Yes," she answered as she placed the gun barrel across the log. "I'm ready."

With that, Morgan raised up and fired at the hiding Ute. "Come on, Dawg," he said, as he broke for the trees at a dead run, while Rose snapped off the four shots. The man and the dog just made the trees as a bullet from Two Bears whined through the tree branches above his head.

"Okay, Dawg, go get him," he ordered. The dog took off running through the trees that would take him around the end of the meadow and on the side where his foe was waiting. Morgan worked his way around to a point where he could see Rose and at the same time, have a good view of the spot where Two Bears was hiding. Crawling up behind some oak brush he stuck the barrel of his rifle through the branches of the oaks and waited for the dog to make his move. He wanted to be ready because the last thing he wanted was for that dog to get hurt. He had to wait for what seemed like an eternity but there was no movement by the Ute. The black horse was in plain sight of the man, but he couldn't see any sign of the Indian or the dog.

Meanwhile, Blue, who had been standing behind the large pine, moved out into the open. This caught the attention of Two Bears. He couldn't believe his eyes. Was that the strange-colored horse his grandfather had told him about? There couldn't be two of them, could there? Was this the white man who had saved the life of his grandfather several years ago? These thoughts puzzled Two

Bears. In fact, he was so busy looking at Blue that he didn't see the dog sneaking up on him.

He's sure taking his sweet time stalking him, Morgan thought to himself.

All of a sudden, all hell broke loose on the other side of the meadow. The Indian had worked his way up the edge of the clearing about fifty feet, evidently trying to get a better look at the odd colored horse. The dog had done a good job of stalking and by the time the Ute saw him and whirled around to fire his rifle, the dog had him by the wrist, his mouth clamped tight. Standing straight up, he gave Morgan the opportunity he was looking for. Aiming his rifle, he pulled the trigger, just as the Ute flung the dog off. Two Bears was hurled to the ground from the recoil of the bullet hitting him. Jumping to his feet, he headed for the black horse, holding his rifle in one hand and grabbing his bleeding side with the other, the dog right behind him. Leaping on his horse and reining him around, he took off through the heavy timber. Morgan ran up just before he disappeared and fired another shot as the rider disappeared from his view. Then whistling the dog back, Morgan ran across to where Rose was standing.

"Did you get him?" she asked, still holding the Colt in her hand.

"Yes," he said hurriedly, taking the gun from her and holstering it, "but he's not dead. Let's get out of here fast in case there are others around."

It didn't take long before Morgan had Rose sitting in the saddle ready to go. By the time the dog came panting up, Morgan had lifted the deer up on Millie's back, strapping him secure with a rope. Then swinging up behind it, he headed through the trees, motioning for Rose to follow. They headed home at a fast pace, keeping well hidden in the trees. When they finally came to the little stream that emptied into the river just above camp, Morgan stopped and, getting off Millie, picked the dog up and put him across the saddle in front of Rose.

"Don't want any dog tracks for them to follow the rest of the way home."

Taking the lead, Morgan started towards the river, carefully staying in the stream and, upon reaching the river, they stayed in the running water. In a short time they crossed over and went downstream towards the camp. Soon they were home safe and sound. It was still daylight and Morgan wanted to get supper over before dark. The first thing he did was to hang the deer in the cottonwood tree next to the cave's entrance. As he built a small fire, Rose said she'd fix something simple to eat. While she was doing that, he unsaddled Blue and rubbed the horses down.

"Will he come after us?" Rose asked as she dished up some food.

"If he's able," he replied. "Took a pretty nasty hit in the side the first shot, and the second, I just don't know. I doubt very seriously if he dies. It's pretty hard to kill a determined man, but it may be a few days before he can ride and begin looking for us. Do you feel up to the ride home?" he asked as he polished off the last bit of food on his plate.

"I think so," she answered. "I'm feeling fine."

"It'll take two or three days to get everything ready. I'll start on the meat in the morning and maybe you and the dog can keep a look-out from the willow for our friend in case I've misjudged him. I know one thing for sure. It's going to take him a while to find us."

****

Two Bears' only thought was to get away so he could sort things out. Pausing at a safe distance, he checked his side. It was not a severe wound and it hadn't damaged any internal organs, but it had torn up his muscles toward his back and would need attention soon. He decided to take a chance and go to the camp where his mother and grandfather were. She would tend to his wound and he needed to talk these things over with his grandfather. This might be the man who had helped his grandfather, and that thought troubled him. Did he avenge himself on an enemy or honor his grandfather's word of peace toward him? He was caught in a dilemma.

Eight

He figured it would be a good night to move out. The moon would be full and since there had been few clouds in the sky the night before, there was a good chance tonight would be clear. So far the day had been pleasantly warm, so if the weather held, it would be a perfect night to go.

The past few days he had done a lot of thinking—debating whether to leave in the daytime or go at night. In the daylight they faced the chance of running into the tall Ute on the black horse. He also had to consider the fact that there had been a Ute encampment about ten miles down the valley when he had arrived a month or so ago. He had no way of knowing what effect the woman's kidnapping had had on the white man's relationship with the Indians. There was the possibility that the Utes in the encampment might be sympathetic towards the renegades. But that was speculation. He wasn't even sure if the Utes were still in the area.

He decided not to take any chances. They would leave during the night when the moon was full and that way the trail would be clear. A slow pace would be best, considering that she hadn't recovered completely and it seemed to him that she was still on the weak side. In the long run a day or two wouldn't make any difference.

That morning at breakfast, Morgan had told Rose his plans. She seemed to take the news with mixed emotions. Naturally she was anxious to get home, to see her family and let them know she was safe but, at the same time, she hated to leave the peace she had found here in this mountainous retreat. Or was it Morgan she would miss the most? She knew it would be hard for Morgan to leave off roaming the mountains. It seemed like the two of them went together, hand in hand, the mountains and the man.

Morgan spent the day packing and cleaning up the camp. By the time he had brushed down the horses it was early afternoon. Since everything was pretty well ready to go, he took Rose and went down to the river to catch some trout for their last meal at the camp. There wasn't too much said as they ate their meal. She had jokingly said she had never eaten so much fish in her whole life but assured him that she loved them and would miss feasting on them when she got home.

"Well, if you miss them too much, you can always go down to the San Juan and catch a mess. If I remember right, you don't live very far from it," Morgan volunteered.

"You're right," she said, "but then I'd have to learn to fish, wouldn't I?"

"Maybe I should come down and teach you!"

"It's a thought," she said with a big smile.

After eating and cleaning up from supper, Rose wandered off into the meadow. After a while Morgan saw her sitting on her favorite stump, dangling her feet in the little stream.

Wonder what she's thinking, he thought. *Wonder if she hates to leave as much as I do?*

She held his gaze for several minutes. She was beautiful sitting there in the fading sunlight, a breeze gently tugging at her hair. It was a sight that would be burned into his memory for a long time. Finally, walking out to where she was, he spoke.

"I hate to break into your thoughts," he said, "but I think you'd better catch a quick nap before we leave."

"You're right," she replied. With that, she went back to her bedroll, which Morgan had left till last to pack and soon she was peacefully sleeping. There was a period of stillness as the sun slipped behind the mountain. The gentle afternoon that had caressed the land quietly gave in to the twilight of the evening. The night creatures were starting their daily chorus. The cooing of the doves was being replaced by the songs of the frogs and crickets that had awoken from their daytime slumber. The moon was just beginning to break over the eastern horizon.

"Wake up, sleepyhead, it's time," Morgan said as he poured the last bit of coffee from his cup and placed it in the pack already on Millie's back. Gathering up her bedroll, he tied it snugly on top of the pack and everything was ready to go. Raking dirt with the side of his boot, he covered the cook fire, firmly tapping it out. Rose had walked to the edge of the meadow and was staring out into the falling darkness. Then Morgan gently touched her shoulder, a touch she knew meant he was ready to leave. She turned and they walked back to the horses as one tear followed by another fell from her eyes.

"I'll never forget this place," she sighed, wiping them away.

"I hope you'll never forget," he said softly. "Maybe someday you can return, you know, for a visit."

They had reached the horses. "Cheer up," Morgan encouraged, and then to reassure her, "you'll be home in no time now."

"I know and I'm so happy about that, but I wish we could stay just one more day," she said wistfully.

"Me, too," he agreed, "but tonight is the perfect time to leave. We have a full moon and a clear sky. It'll be almost like daylight. This way, we won't take a chance of running into Two Bears and if the Ute encampment is still there we can slip by it and still have time to cross back across the river. We'll rest tomorrow and leave early the next morning. That will give you and the horses some time to rest up."

Mounting Blue and kicking his boot free of the stirrup, he motioned for her hand. Placing her foot in the stirrup, she swung up behind him.

"Let's go, Dawg," he said and the dog shot through the opening. Morgan nudged the horse forward.

"You're not going to lead Millie?" Rose asked.

"Nope. She trails along pretty good and the dog makes sure she doesn't stray too far. Generally she stays pretty close to Blue.... you need to hang on tight," he reminded Rose as Blue entered the willows. "Put your face up close to my back or else you might get slapped by one of those pesky boughs."

She put her arms around his waist and squeezed herself close to him, and a peaceful feeling of security came over her. She somehow knew everything was going to be all right. Blue reached the river and carefully picked his way across. He kept Blue in the water until he came to the little stream and then he turned and went up it. A hundred yards or so he left it and headed south. The moon was hanging in the night sky like a big round orange as it ascended over the eastern horizon.

"Look at the size of that moon," he said. "Have you ever wondered why it appears so big and bright when it first comes up over the horizon? I have, many times."

"No," she said, "I haven't, but it is beautiful."

It was a stunning night, the air was still and the moon was doing a good job of lighting up the surroundings. As it rose higher in the sky, its rays cast eerie shadows across the terrain. Blue soon came to the game trail that more or less followed the river on its way towards New Mexico. As if talking to himself, Morgan muttered, "We'll follow this trail on down past the Ute camp. A little farther on is a good place to cross back over the river. I know an excellent spot to spend tomorrow on the other side." He turned his head towards the woman behind him. "You'll tell me if you start getting tired or sore and we can stop and rest or walk awhile."

"I'm fine," she replied. "Maybe later it would be nice to walk for awhile. It's so lovely out tonight and not nearly as cold as I thought it might be." For some time they rode in silence, the dog was up front, then Blue with his two passengers and trudging behind with head drooped low was Millie. "You know, it's awfully hard for me to see anything ahead of us," she whispered in his ear. "You are tall and broad, you know."

"Well now, I can fix that," he replied, bringing Blue to a stop. Swinging his leg forward over the saddle horn, he slid to the ground. "Now you sit yourself up there in the saddle." When she had made herself comfortable, he gathered up the reins and handed them to her. Grabbing the saddle horn, he swung up behind her. "Is that better?" he asked.

"You bet," she replied. "I can see everything now."

They rode awhile in silence, enjoying the serenity of the evening. Finally Rose spoke up. "I was just wondering, have you had Dawg a long time?" she asked as she watched the dog stop and wait for them to catch up.

"He's not really mine," was the reply.

"What do you mean, he's not yours?" Before Morgan could answer, she added, "If he's not yours, who does he belong to?"

"Nobody, that I know of. I guess you might say he belongs to himself. He and I just travel together, you know, mutual companionship, sort of a partnership. I cover his back and he covers mine."

"Oh," she said, "but now I'm curious." She turned in the saddle and looked at him. "How did this mutual admiration society get started?"

"Well, it happened the year I wintered at the Fort. They had put me up in a little shack just outside the stockade. It had a small lean-to on the backside to keep my horse out of the weather. Just off the lean-to, maybe thirty feet or so, was a heavy wooded canyon, the oak brush so thick that a man couldn't walk through it. That winter was a bad one. It was cold and it seemed like the wind blew constantly. It made the little storms seem like blizzards. Late one afternoon, I had just come home from a patrol and it was one of those days, overcast and cold, spitting snow and, of course, the wind was blowing. It looked like it was snowing sideways. As I dismounted to lead my horse into the shed...."

"You mean Blue?" she interrupted.

"No, Blue came later, but that's another story. Let's get back to this one. As I dismounted, I noticed a small pup sitting on the edge of the canyon. I led my horse into the shed and unsaddled him and fed him some grain. As I came out I stopped and looked at this ragged little pup. He got up and snarled at me, in a weakly sort of way. Then he started limping towards the brush in the canyon. He was a pitiful sight, dragging one hind leg, his ribs sticking out like he was almost starved to death. I started towards him, but he dragged himself into the brush and disappeared. I don't know where he came from, but it was apparent that something or someone had terribly abused him. To this day he hates men in general, especially soldiers and Indians.

"That evening when I was fixing my supper, I couldn't get that pitiful mutt out of my mind. I can't stand to see an animal suffer needlessly. I cut off an extra elk steak and after it was cooked I cut it into little chunks and put them with a couple of crumbled biscuits on a plate and poured gravy on top. I placed the plate under a branch that hung out so it would have some protection from the snow. The next morning the food was gone, so that night I put some more food out, only I moved the plate closer to the lean-to. In the morning it was gone again. So every night after that I put the food out, setting it closer and closer to the shed each time.

"Some days there was nothing to do, so I stayed around the shack. I could see him laying at the edge of the brush so I would sit on the porch and talk to him. Eventually I worked him up to the lean-to by putting the food just inside. As first he wouldn't stay in during the night, but then I noticed he was sleeping inside with the horse. When I would go outside, he would head for the cover of the thick oak brush. Gradually he would sit at the edge and watch me. Well, this went on for about three months, spring was coming and I had decided I wasn't cut out for Army life. So one March day I quit, packed up my few belongings and was fixing to head out. The dog sat and watched me packing up the horse and it was almost as if he knew somehow that I wasn't coming back this time. As I rode out, he started to follow, hanging back, and in fact most of the time he stayed out of sight. That first night I put his food out, the regular, a piece of meat with biscuits and gravy. The next morning it was gone. I didn't see too much of him that day but that night, on schedule, I put out his regular meal. The next day the meat was still there but the biscuits and gravy were gone. I figured he was hunting on his own now, but he was crazy about my biscuits and gravy and couldn't resist them."

"Well, I agree with him there," she said. "Your biscuits and gravy are *good*!"

"I kept feeding him his favorite food and then one morning I woke up and he was sleeping in the camp. As time went on, we became good buddies, trusting each other and watching each other's back. He's a great partner and he can smell a human a mile away. Even when he's sleeping, it's like he still hears everything going on around him. He's warned me many a time and even pulled me out of a scary scrape or two, as you know. In fact, if it hadn't been for him, I don't know if I could have gotten you away from those Utes."

They had come to the top of the ridge. The trail sloped gently downward until it reached the river far below. "This would be a good time to walk a spell." Blue stopped as if he knew exactly what the man had said.

"I am getting a little stiff," Rose said, as Morgan dismounted and helped her to the ground.

"That Ute camp is at the bottom, oh, two or three miles at the most. We'll walk until we're almost to it and then we'll ride as quietly as we can to get past it." As an afterthought, Morgan assured her that if she got tired before that, she could ride if she wanted to.

The moon was high in the sky now. The landscape was lit up as bright as day. Walking to the edge of the trail and looking over, she could see the river far below. It was like a long glittering ribbon weaving back and forth in the night as the moonlight reflected off the water. Morgan joined her and for a few minutes they took in the beauty of the night. In the spell of the moment, they could hear the sounds in the dark. The breeze was gently rustling through the aspen trees behind them on the hillside. In the distance the lonesome sound of a hoot owl drifted from the canyon below, blending with the song of the crickets in the thicket of spruce trees growing just below the trail.

"Look!" Morgan said, breaking the quiet. "See that herd of elk in the clearing just to the left of the bend in the river?"

"No, I don't," she replied, looking hard at the terrain below. "Where?"

"To the left," he repeated. "Let me show you." Reaching down, he took her hand and pointed in the direction of the herd.

"Okay, I see them now," she said. "You'll have to excuse me. I'm not used to sight-seeing in the middle of the night."

It suddenly dawned on him that he was still holding her hand and reluctantly, he released it. He had a funny feeling in the pit of his stomach, a feeling he had never felt before. He would have liked to hold her hand longer, but thought better ot it.

"We'd better get going," he said, trying to get his mind on something else.

Starting down the trail, the dog took the lead. Morgan started in behind him. Rose stepped up and, taking him by the arm, fell in beside him. "I don't want to fall," she said teasingly. Old Blue, with his reins tied up over his neck, fell in behind, followed by

Millie. They had walked a little while when she spoke up.

"I just don't remember!"

"Don't remeber what?" he asked, puzzled by what she meant.

"I don't remember a thing about the night you rescued me. I know you've told me, but I've tried and tried and I just can't remember. I remember being on the Indian pony and wishing I was dead, but the next thing I knew I was waking up in your camp."

For the next few minutes they reminisced about the rescue. She laughed when he came to the part about coming face to face with the missing Indian. When Morgan finished, Rose, walking faster, caught up with the dog and, kneeling down, she hugged him and whispered *thank you* in his ear. When Morgan caught up she took his arm once more.

"I am sorry you both got hurt that night."

"We're fine," he assured her. "We only got scratched up some. We're in great shape now."

They walked in silence for quite a long while, both lost in thought. She wondered if her life would ever be the same. In a way she had become attatched to this man and it was like he was a part of her now. She had come to depend so much on him and she had such a feeling of security when he was near. It was a comfortable feeling that she didn't look forward to losing. At the same time, he was thinking that he would surely miss her. He had enjoyed taking care of her and it gave him a good feeling to be responsible for someone. He dreaded the time when he would have to say good-bye—when he would again feel that awful loneliness that had been his lot in life for the past eleven years.

Suddenly it dawned on him where they were. Stopping the group, he decided it was time to get ready to ride past the camp.

First he dug out a lead rope from the pack and put it on Millie's halter. He didn't want her wandering around when they passed by. Then, putting Rose on the horse behind him and holding firmly to the lead rope, they started down the trail again.

"Let's be as quiet as possible," he whispered. "And if you horses let out one peep, I'll have you for dinner, understand?"

As they broke out of the trees they caught sight of the Ute encampment. It was down and across a little valley. There were about a dozen teepees set up on the east bank of the river. There was a thick growth of spruce trees on the south side of the settlement and on the west, forming a sort of triangle, was a small stream that emptied into the river just below the teepees. The horses were tethered down the slope a bit from the dwellings in a small aspen grove. Morgan gave a piercing glance to see if there might be a big black among them, but he really couldn't tell whether they were black or brown. He guessed it really didn't matter anyway.

The only thing stirring was an occasional wisp of smoke swirling up from a few dying campfires. Everything else seemed quiet. Morgan eased Blue down along the trail when suddenly, about half-way down, a dog started yelping from the camp. Halting the group behind a growth of oak brush, he motioned for them to be very quiet. Dismounting, he worked his way around the brush so he could watch the camp to make sure nobody was alerted. The dog quieted down and he saw no evidence of movement out of any of the teepees. Returning, he quietly told them that they should wait a while to make sure everything had settled down. In about twenty minutes, he nudged Blue and they went on to the bottom without attracting any more attention. Here they crossed a small stream and angled back behind a growth of spruce that hid them from view of the Indian camp. Morgan sighed a sigh of relief. The trail now started up-hill once more and at the top of the first ridge, he stopped to take the lead rope off Millie and give the horses a breather.

"Just a couple of miles more," he told her as he helped her off the horse. "We'll cross back over the river and from there it's not too far to a place I know where we can spend tomorrow and tomorrow night." After stretching and walking for a few minutes, he helped her back on Blue. "Are you getting tired?"

"I'm tired and a little stiff, but I'll be all right." She yawned and slightly leaned back on his chest.

"Well, you can sleep all day tomorrow and all night if you want to. If you're still tired we'll stay as long as it takes to get you rested." With that they started on down the trail towards the river.

Morgan was a little concerned about the tracks they were leaving. Chances were that the Utes would not even notice them on the trail. If they did notice, they might feel inclined to ignore them, thinking they were made by a prospector passing through. There was an outside chance they would be curious. In that case he would hide their trail the best he could and maybe that would discourage any following of them. In any case, the Indians probably could care less about this little group on their way home. What he couldn't understand was why he had started worrying so much about things. Was it because of Rose?

Soon they came to the place where a good sized creek ran into the Piedra. Stopping, he laid the dog across the saddle in front of Rose. Mounting once more, they started down the middle of the creek. Soon they came to the river, which was wider and fairly shallow and Morgan felt it was a good place to cross. Once on the other side, he stayed in the water at the edge for a hundred yards or so. Then cutting up a ravine that was hidden by a brush growth, they started their climb out of the river bottom. The rode for a couple of hours—the moon had gone down in the west and the sky was starting to lighten up in the east.

"Hang on, guys, we're almost there," he said cheerfully as he saw light breaking through the trees ahead.

****

Morgan had been sure when they passed by the Indian camp that no one had noticed, but that was not the case. There had been an interested pair of eyes following their progress as they descended down towards the camp. He had watched as they paused, hidden from view, waiting for the dog to quit barking. His eyes were glued on them as they came down, crossed the creek, and disappeared from his sight.

Not being able to sleep, Two Bears had wandered out by the stream. Sitting on a rock under the spreading limb of a spruce tree, he was once more trying to sort out the troubling thoughts that kept running through his mind. He was undecided as to what he was going to do about this white man. He wanted so badly to kill him and recover the woman. Yet was he honor-bound to abide by his grandfather's wishes to protect him? He cared nothing for the white man but he respected and loved his grandfather very much. On the other hand, he had to think about his pride. Others had seen this man take his prize away from him and his humiliation at being hit in the face. Then there was the wound that he was recovering from now. His family and friends knew how he had left himself open to being shot. Granted, it wasn't a life-threatening wound, but it was embarrassing to say the least. In the last several days he and his grandfather had spent many hours talking about the events of the previous few weeks. The old man had tried to make it clear that he disliked the white man in general as much as Two Bears did. However it was their world now and to resist the system would only bring more hurt and misery to his people. Two Bears needed to think about his future. The white woman was back in her world now and if she was left alone, maybe the whole affair would be forgotten.

The trouble was, Two Bears had no intention of making peace with his white enemies. He would not surrender to the enemy of his people even if it cost him his life. This newest enemy was a different matter. There was more involved than two different cultures. This was a matter of honor. He knew what he must do first. He would follow them and when he came to a decision, he would act. At daybreak he asked his mother to dress his wound once more and when this was done, he gathered his things together, his blanket, food and ammunition, and said farewell to his family, mounting the black as he started what may be his final hunt.

Morgan wasn't the easiest man to track but the Indian was patient. He didn't figure the white man would stay on the trail. That would be the simplest thing to do, but Two Bears had a gut feeling this man would play it safe and cut across to Durango, using the game trails and stream bottoms. The thought crossed his mind that since they rode all night that they would hole up to rest, so they had to be somewhere in the immediate vicinity. Keeping his eyes peeled on the west side of the trail, he looked for signs of two horses and a dog.

The tracking had gotten slow, the trail being very hard and rocky. When Two Bears got to the creek he went on up the trail. As it started through a stand of aspens, the ground softened up and it was then that he could not find their tracks. For sure there were no dog tracks. He had missed them somewhere back down the trail. He had a good idea where they had turned off the creek and, backtracking, he went down the stream, but no tracks on either side indicated where they had gone. Maybe he had been wrong. Maybe they had left the trail at another place or maybe they crossed the river, but then they could have gone either upstream or down. Which was it? He had no idea. There were several places Morgan could have climbed out of the river bed, so he would simply have to keep looking until he found their tracks. Searching for a couple of hours, Two Bears finally picked up the tracks and started to follow his prey.

Nine

The morning sun was hitting the tops of the western peaks as they broke out of the trees. Before them lay a huge meadow, a large part of which was covered by beaver dams. These dams were fed by a sizeable stream running out of a large valley covered with aspen trees. This provided plenty of food and water for a good sized colony of beavers.

"Goodness," Rose exclaimed. "Never in my whole life have I seen so many beaver in one place."

"It's a big one, all right," replied the man as he turned the horses up along the edge of the spruce trees bordering the clearing, "and it's got fish in it too." He knew exactly where he was headed—an overhanging rock that would provide adequate shelter and protection. If they needed to leave in a hurry, there were several ways they could go. There was plenty of tall grass for Blue and Millie to graze on and still be out of sight.

"I'll get some wood for a cook fire," Rose offered, "while you take care of the horses."

"Fine," Morgan said, "but make sure it's good and dry. We want to keep the smoke down as much as possible."

As soon as she had the fire started, she put the coffee pot on. In the meantime Morgan pulled the packs off Millie and staked her out to graze. Unsaddling Blue, he staked him away from Millie a bit and after brushing both of them down, he returned to the fire. After breakfast and while Rose was washing the dishes in one of the ponds, Morgan cut an armload of the tall grass and made a comfortable mattress to put her bedroll on. Laying down on her newly made bed, she couldn't remember when anything had felt so good. She realized she was more exhausted than she wanted to admit and was soon fast asleep.

Finding a higher place overlooking their camp and the beaver ponds, Morgan spent the morning dozing and keeping watch just in case someone might have picked up their trail and was following them. The dog spent his time surveying the surrounding area, periodically coming in and taking a nap at the foot of the woman's bed. It was a lazy, sunny day with a few scattered clouds floating slowly across the sky. Now and then a gentle breeze would blow through the huge groves of aspen trees that surrounded the ponds. There was nothing in the world, the man thought, like those rustling leaves to put a fellow to sleep. The aspens were just starting to change color. Soon there would be huge patches of golden yellow, giving the mountains a giant checker-board effect.

As the afternoon wore on, he couldn't help noticing the trout in the ponds, rising to take flies off the surface of the water. They would make a tasty supper, he thought. Getting his fishing line, he carefully crept up behind a big pine tree that had fallen out across one of the dams. Flipping a big ol' grasshopper over the log and into the water, he barely had time to lean back when he caught a nice one. The fish in the ponds were not as big as the ones in the river, but they were still good eating. Soon he had enough for a meal. After cleaning them, he started up the small fire and put supper on. When everything was ready he woke Rose.

"Are you going to sleep all day?" he asked.

"I guess," she said, yawning. "I didn't realize how tired I was and stiff and sore in a certain area!"

Morgan laughed. "You'll toughen up in a day or two and by the time we get home, you'll be as tough as saddle leather. In the meantime, let's get some food in you and then we'll walk some of the soreness out."

Twilight was starting to fall by the time they had eaten, cleaned up, and taken a walk around the ponds. Returning, Morgan gathered up Blue and Millie, leading them to the pond for their nightly drink. While the horses were in the process of snorting and drinking their fill, Rose wandered up and was brushing flies off Blue's back.

"You know," she commented, "he's sure an odd colored horse."

And it was true. His coloring was a light bluish gray dapple and in the right light he looked blue. A little white star adorned his forehead and his legs faded into white stockings. His body was short and stocky with powerful shoulders and legs. His head appeared small for the size of his body. Though he wasn't the best looking horse in the world, he had an easy gait and could cover ground like no other. It was his endurance that Morgan had come to appreciate and depend on.

"I've never seen another one quite like him," Morgan said and then chuckled. "You ought to see him when he has his long winter coat. But all kidding aside, he's a good horse—stout and strong-winded. He and I have covered a lot of territory in the past few years. He doesn't get excited even though he has a lot of spirit. Learns fast and has never given me any trouble. We work well together."

"And I suppose there's a story on how you two met?"

"Yes, as a matter of fact, there is, and I suppose you want to hear it."

"Do I have a choice?" she asked teasingly.

"No," he retorted. "Besides, we need to talk about something this evening, don't we?"

Leading the horses back and staking them out for the night, the man and woman settled down by the embers of the dying fire. It was dark now and the full moon was rising. But tonight there were clouds drifting by and at times they were blocking the brightness of the moon and bathing the earth in a gentle darkness.

"Well, let's hear the story," she said impatiently as she handed him a hot cup of coffee.

Settling back for a few minutes, Morgan's mind went back to the events that led up to him getting Blue on that late spring morning down in the foothills of the San Juans.

"Rose, do you remember me telling you about leaving the Fort and Dawg followed me?"

"Yes, I remember," she said. "After all, it was just last night!"

"You know, you're right. It *was* last night. Well, let me continue with the tale then. The dog and I had only been out about two months. We had gone to higher elevations but there was still so much snow that we wandered back down into the foothills. Topping a little ridge one morning, I saw a commotion going on down in a meadow. Looked like two men were having a knockdown, drag-out brawl. Generally I ride around other people's difficulties and mind my own business, but something about this fight didn't look exactly fair. As I rode down towards them, I noticed several horses, but the only men I could see were the two involved in the fighting. As I got closer, I could see that a big, strapping white man was beating the stuffing out of an old Indian. It made me mad instantly and as I rode up, I yelled at the big guy to let him loose. He dropped the old man and turned towards me. 'I suppose you're gonna make me', he said with a big sneer on his face. 'I just might do exactly that,' I told him in a low, calm voice as I dismounted and faced him. 'Now back away from the old man.'

"Just then, out of the corner of my eye, I caught sight of another *hombre* who had a rifle aimed right at me. It was cocked and I had an awful feeling that he was getting ready to pull the trigger. A cold chill ran down my spine. *Morgan, why can't you just mind your own business,* I thought. I was desperately trying to decide what to do when a furry ball of dog came flying through the air, landing right in the middle of the man with the rifle. The rifle went off and the bullet zinged over the top of my head. The big man went for his gun and I got him with the first shot. Turning, I got the other one with the second shot."

"Did you kill them?" she asked hesitantly.

"I'm afraid so. It happened so fast and I was so mad," he replied, slowly shaking his head. "You know, I've shot several men in my lifetime, but these were the only ones that died. After everything settled down and I had cooled off, I got sick to my stomach."

"Was the old man all right?"

"Yeah, but he was beat up pretty bad. He didn't regain

consciousness for several hours. I fixed a bed for him in the shade and cleaned and put some salve on his cuts and bruises."

"So what happened to the two men? You know, the bodies."

"I buried them along with all their belongings, except the guns and ammunition—I kept them. Figured they owed me something for the aggravation of having to bury them. Digging two graves isn't fun, you know. Oh, and what little money they had, I put in the old Indian's pack."

"You buried all their belongings? Their horses, too?"

"No, silly. You wouldn't catch me digging a hole big enough to bury two horses and, besides, *they* hadn't done anything wrong. I turned them loose and they scooted away. I suppose they went home, wherever that was. But I buried everything else—saddles, bridles, bedrollls, everything. They weren't worth much anyway since they were all worn out."

"Well now, after you disposed of those two, what happened to the old Indian?"

"He finally came to but was very weak. Couldn't even talk for a couple of days. I went out and got a small deer and fixed him up some broth and fed him that for a few days."

"You seem to enjoy helping people in trouble," she said with admiration in her eyes. "How long did you stay with him? Did he get all right?" She asked, still wondering what this had to do with Blue.

"He was a tough old bird and he recovered pretty fast. Didn't talk much, though. I could understand some of his lingo, but not much. He didn't savvy any English but we didn't have much to talk about anyway. In about a week, four Indian bucks came riding up, about the time we were eating dinner. They surrounded us and then just sat there on their ponies staring down at us for what seemed an eternity. I wasn't sure what was going to happen, so I kept my hand away from my six-gun and stayed very still. The old man jumped up and started jabbering to them. In a little while three of them dismounted and two of them began gathering up his things while one went to get his two horses. The other one just sat there on his pony and kept his eyes glued to my every move.

"One of them came up to me leading one of the old man's horses. In broken English he told me that his grandfather wanted me to have this horse. A gift, he said, for saving his life and taking care of him. He advised me that it wouldn't be wise to refuse this gift. The old man began talking to his grandson again and then the young one turned to me and said, 'My grandfather says horse will be good for you, carry you many places, has a brave, strong heart. Be good medicine for you.' Then they put him on his horse and took off."

"That was his way of saying *thank you*, wasn't it?"

"I'm sure it was," Morgan said and then got a silly grin on his face. "But I wish you could have seen this animal! He had to be the ugliest horse I had ever laid eyes on. It was late spring and he hadn't completely shed his winter coat. Part of his hide was slick and shiny but a lot of him was covered with this long, shaggy winter coat. With his bluish gray coloring, dappled with white, he had more white on him than he does now. He looked like one of my mother's old quilts she used to have on one of our beds.

"The first thing I did was to get the curry comb and give him a good brushing and that helped a little. I could tell he hadn't been broke to ride yet, even though he was fairly gentle. I tied him up close to the camp and spent most of the evening just sitting there looking at him, trying to figure out what I was going to do with the world's ugliest horse."

"Well, I know you kept him," she replied.

"He grows on you," he said in return. "I spent a big part of that summer breaking him to ride. I have this thing about being bucked off, so I took my time. First I got him used to the bridle and then I put my saddle on him until it didn't bother him any longer. Then I gradually tied weight on the saddle until he got used to that. One afternoon I swung aboard him and he pranced around some, but didn't buck once. I found out he was very smart and it didn't take long until he was a first-class pony. I started riding him and leading my other horse. I was impressed by his strength and the smoothness of his gait and he was so easy to ride, could turn on a dime and had the surefootedness that a horse needs in the mountains. There was a bond that developed between us, sort of like me and the dog. When I got back to Animas City that fall, I saw Milllie and knew she was the pack animal I needed. So I traded the Sorrell for her and made fifty bucks to boot. The four of us have been together ever since."

"I think you make a wonderful team, myself," she said. "You for sure saved my life and I'm grateful to all of you." With that, she gave the dog another big hug.

"I still can't believe how that dog took to you. You're the only person, besides myself, who has been able to get close to him." Putting his cup away, Morgan added, "I reckon it's time to turn in. We need to get an early start tomorrow."

"How far do you think we'll get?" she wanted to know.

"Oh, we'll get to the Pine River, at least."

"Boy, there's sure a lot of rivers in this part of the country," she said, shaking her head.

"Yes," he replied, "there's six just between Pagosa and the La Plata mountains on the west side of Durango. The San Juan headwaters above Pagosa and runs down towards your ranch. Then there's the Piedra, where my camp was. Tomorrow we'll be at the Pine and, hopefully, the Florida the next day. Durango is on the Animas and finally there's the La Plata River to the west."

"What's the Pine River like?" she asked.

"It's a lot like the Piedra. It is formed by two streams coming together high in the foothills. The other stream is the Vallecito. The Indians called it the *Los Piños*. I've explored most of it but there's places not accessible to man or horse. It runs south and empties into the San Juan River a few miles south of the Colorado-New Mexico line."

"Will we camp there tomorrow night?" Rose asked in the midst of a rather large yawn.

"Maybe, depending on the time of day. We'll see. But now, young lady, it's time to hit the old bedroll. You're about to go to sleep on your feet," Morgan said, as he started to fix his own bedroll for the night.

"I guess you're right," Rose said, as she snuggled down in her blankets. "Are you going to tuck me in?" she asked, giggling.

"No way!" Morgan said with a final note. "G'night, Roseanna, see you in the morning."

****

The sun had been up for a couple of hours by the time Two Bears approached the meadow. He figured it would be the place the white man would stop and rest. He had to be careful, as he didn't want to reveal his presence just yet. The wind was blowing from the northwest so, staying well back from the beaver dams, he circled to the southeast. He couldn't afford to let the dog get his scent. There was a high ridge running east and west, just south of his quarry. Keeping high and well hidden in the trees, Two Bears finally located Morgan's camp. Although it was a good distance away, he could still make out some of the activity. He could see the horses and as long as they were there, so was his enemy—or friend. He still hadn't decided which it was. Staking the big black in some tall grass far enough away so he couldn't catch the scent of the other horses, he settled down in the shade of a spruce tree and watched the activities going on below him.

Ten

It was breaking light when Morgan got up and started a fire, putting the coffee on. By the time breakfast was over and the horses packed, the rays of the morning sun were peeking over the mountain top and slowly creeping down the tree covered slopes of the western ridges. Leaving the camp, they circled the beaver ponds on the southern end and there Morgan picked his way up the mountain side following an old game trail.

"After we work our way over this ridge, there's one more," he explained. "Then we should find one of the trails to Durango. We'll make the Pine River by mid-afternoon and maybe we should stay there tonight. I know a beautiful spot."

It was mid-morning when they found the trail they needed to take them home. It was almost level for the next couple of miles so Morgan and Rose decided to walk for awhile. As the trail started uphill again, Morgan put Rose on Blue but he decided to walk a bit further. They paused at the top of a short incline, the trail continuing to wind downwards in and out of the trees on its way to the bottom of a deep canyon. Suddenly Blue's and Millie's heads went up, ears perked forward and Blue uttered a low snort. The dog had also stopped and was staring down in the canyon, a warning growl rumbling from his throat.

"Something or someone's coming," Morgan muttered. "I can't make anything out yet, so we better stay put for a moment and see who it is." Walking up beside Blue, who intently watched the trail, Morgan gently took the reins. They stood there fixed to the spot for a few minutes. Then Morgan moved Blue off the trail, turning him so the man could stand squarely in front of Rose sitting in the saddle. That way he would be facing anyone who came up the trail. Millie stopped right behind Blue, still straining her ears toward the sound she was hearing. The dog had scurried down the trail a few feet and had sat down on the edge, staring straight down toward the noise.

Morgan started to say something to Rose when his eye caught the slight movement of a horse coming through the trees. Then a horse and rider broke out in the open, followed by two more riders. As they became visible, the dog scooted off into the brush along the trail. Morgan instinctively put his hand to his side, resting the palm of his hand on the front of his holster.

"Everyone stay calm and let's see who our friends are," Morgan said in a low, calm voice. He was silent for a moment and then Rose heard him say, 'Oh, no!' under his breath.

"You know these men?" she whispered.

"Yep, afraid so, at least the one in front," he whispered back.

He recognized the man in front as a ruffian called 'Crazy' Bill Whiting. Morgan didn't know the two men following him, though he did recognize their type. *That* wasn't the best of news! He remembered Bill Whiting, all right. He was kind of a likable man, with a weird sense of humor, that is when he wasn't riled up over something. Six-foot-one, he was a handsome sort, with a slender build. He wore a black Stetson hat tipped back on his head. He wore his gun on the right and Morgan remembered that he knew how to use it. He had come by his name because of his short fuse and when he lost his temper, he would throw a crazy fit. You couldn't believe a word he said and only a fool would turn his back to him. Another thing that came to mind was that he was always ready to make an easy buck and wasn't particular how he did it.

"Well, well, if it isn't Fletcher Morgan," was Whiting's greeting as he reined in his horse about fifteen feet from Morgan. "I haven't seen you for quite a spell."

"Hello, Bill. It's been three, maybe four years, I reckon."

"Hey, boys, this gent is Fletcher Morgan," Whiting said. "He and I used to work together for some of the mines up Silverton way. He's real handy with that six-shooter. Yes, sir, *real* handy!" Turning in his saddle he motioned toward the men behind him. "Morgan, these two fellows are friends of mine. This here is Charlie Banks and the one in the rear is his brother, Tom."

"Howdy," Morgan said as he studied the two, keeping an eye on Crazy Bill. It didn't take long to size up the other two—real dregs of mankind. They looked like they'd cut your throat for two bits.

Charlie Banks was a short, heavy-set man who looked about forty years old. He wore an old hat that drooped down over his left ear. Most of the features of his face were hid by a beard that was unkempt and when he said hello to Morgan and smiled, it was evident that someone had knocked out one of his upper front teeth. His clothes were worn and looked like they hadn't been washed in a coon's age. He wore an old beat-up revolver on the right side and on the left was the biggest hunting knife Morgan had ever seen. He looked like he'd be a hard man to beat in a fist fight.

Tom Banks, on the other hand, was younger and taller and not quite as heavy as Charlie. He was clean shaven and wore a fairly nice hat. His clothes were cleaner and neater than those of his brother. He wore a nice-looking six-gun on the left side. He didn't crack a smile when he acknowledged Morgan with just a nod. He had the eyes of a cold-blooded killer. Focusing his attention back to Bill Whiting, Morgan addressed him.

"What you been up to, Bill? Anything useful?"

"Nothing worth bragging about. Right now we're on our way to Pagosa Springs to see an old boy who's looking for some help. If that doesn't work out, we figured on taking some baths and relaxing for a spell."

That's a laugh, Morgan thought to himself. There must be something else up—someone must have died for the vultures to be out like this.

Whiting lifted his left leg out of the stirrup and slung it over the saddle horn and kind of sat sideways in the saddle. Taking his fixings out of his shirt pocket, he proceeded to roll himself a smoke. "Well, Morgan, aren't you going to introduce us to the young lady? Don't tell me you went and took yourself a wife!" He winked as he said it. Before Morgan could say anything, Rose spoke up.

"My name is Roseanna Jackson and no, we're not married."

There was silence for a moment before Whiting spoke again. "Roseanna Jackson? Well, well, well." Turning, he said to the men with him, "Boys, this little lady is Roseanna Jackson. Say *howdy* to her."

Tom Banks didn't say anything, just stared at her, but brother Charlie, with a wide grin exposing his missing tooth said, "Pleased to meet ya, ma'am!"

Turning back to face Morgan, Whiting, with a big grin on his face, said in a congratulatory way, "I got to hand it to you, Morgan, you sure know how to find the pot of gold at the end of the rainbow."

"What on earth are you talking about?" Morgan shot back.

"Why, this little lady is famous. Her family has the whole country looking for her. Why, they even got the army involved! Every rock in the territory is being turned over to find her. What's more, she valuable, too. There's a thousand dollar reward for the person finding her and returning her home."

Then laughing and winking at Morgan, he continued, "What are you going to do with all that money?"

"A thousand dollars!" gasped Rose.

"You've *got* to be kidding!" Morgan stammered.

"Nope, it's a fact. And you're the lucky one who hit the jackpot. Old Man Jackson is just going to love you to pieces!"

"If you're right and everyone's out looking for her, why haven't we seen anybody?" Morgan asked him.

"Well, I guess," Whiting said, "because they didn't figure she'd be this far south and west. The day she was snatched, army patrol out of Pagosa picked up the trail of the renegades who they assumed had her. That was on the east side of the Piedra and they were headed in a northeasterly direction. The soldier boys chased after them, hopeful they still had Miss Jackson, here, and that she was all right. They sent a man back to Pagosa," he continued, "to get more help and I understand that when he got there, he ran into two of the Jackson brothers and some of the men they had with them."

"My brothers were looking for me?" Rose asked.

"Yes, ma'am and I believe they're still out looking. A good number of men took out in that direction also, most of them out for the money. Someone told me that another troop of soldiers left Fort Lewis, too. I don't know where you two have been hiding to miss all the folks that's been looking for you."

"Did they catch the Indians?" Morgan inquired.

"Some of them. The posse caught up with about half a dozen of them and in the shoot-out, one Ute was killed, two were shot up, and one got away. The boys and I figured we could use that money so we got in the thick of the chase, too. We got there after that first fun battle. The Jackson boys and a few others had taken out after the one who escaped. With so many more men being added to the search, there was no way of knowing who's tracks were who's and we finally got disgusted and went back to Durango. About two days ago when we left Durango to check out this job in Pagosa, we heard they were still looking for the last Ute. What is interesting," Whiting mused, "is all these Indians swear that a white man stole the woman from them and that she was all right when they last saw her. Nobody believed them, thought they were lying, but they weren't, were they? The Jacksons couldn't find any sign of their sister and they're still out hunting. Everyone else assumes that if the lady is alive and the Indians are right, she would still be with this white guy. Most folks are of the mind that she's dead and they've given up the search. Now, look, here she is, alive and well and on her way home with a white man, just like the Indians said."

Rose started to say something about the last Ute, but decided against it when she saw the look in Morgan's eyes.

"Yeah, we're on the way home," Morgan said, trying to change the subject. "Shouldn't take over three days at the most."

"Before you go," Whiting said, "you got to tell me how you stole her from those red devils. I bet you had a fight on your hands. Did you have to shoot anyone?"

"No, I didn't shoot anyone. I just sneaked into their camp after dark and took her. Then we hid until she had recovered enough to take the ride home."

"You mean they just let you walk in and take her? That's hard to believe, Morgan."

"Well, to tell the truth, they were drunk and it wasn't that hard," Morgan replied, not wanting to go into any more details.

"Well, don't let us hold you up....better get her on home," Whiting said as he swung his leg back down and put his boot in the stirrup. "We'll be on our way. Glad to see you're well, ma'am. Real glad!"

With that, Whiting and the Banks brothers nudged their horses and continued on in the direction that Morgan and Rose had just come from. Charlie tipped his old hat and smiled at Rose as he passed, but there was no acknowledgement by Tom Banks.

'Thank you for letting us know," Rose said as the three of them passed by.

Morgan stood and watch the trio as they disappeared down into the trees. Swinging up behind Rose, he started Blue down the trail with Millie falling in behind. The dog came out of the brush and took his customary place just in front of the lead horse.

"I wish my family knew I was safe," Rose said wistfully. After a long pause, she added, "If there were so many people looking for me, I wonder why we didn't see someone."

"It's easy, really," Morgan answered. "First of all, we were in an out-of-the-way place and pretty well hid to boot. Secondly, it rained so hard that night I took you from them, it more than likely removed all the tracks leading to my place. When the posse found the Ute tracks it was several miles from where we were. They headed northwest and the posse probably assumed you were still with them. Maybe I should have run the posse down that day I went out and told them where you were, but I was afraid to leave you by yourself that long. I couldn't have caught up with them and got back by nightfall anyway. You would have had to spend the night with only the dog for company."

"No," she assured him, shaking her head. "You did the right thing. I wasn't up to traveling at that time and I was afraid and nervous all the time you were gone."

They rode in silence, but Morgan was deep in thought. He didn't trust Whiting and his friends as far as he could toss a range bull. He knew Bill was greedy and that he didn't care how he got what he wanted. He wanted Rose, she was worth a lot of money to him, and Morgan had seen the greed in his eyes when he was talking to Rose. One thing for sure, they hadn't seen the last of those three. He wasn't going to say anything to Rose, but he had to figure out a way to get them to come to him on his terms, not theirs. To wait for them to make their move would make him and Rose sitting ducks. How could he draw them out and be ready for them?

Looking up at the sky, he figured it was noon. Since Rose had the reins, he asked her to stop in a little clearing where a small brook crossed the trail. "We'll stop for a short rest and make a pot of coffee. We'll make the river about three o'clock this afternoon and then we'll stop there and cook an early supper and maybe spend the night, depending on how tired you are at that time."

Swinging down off Blue, he helped Rose down. She stretched

and walked down by the brook to loosen up her stiff joints. After loosening the saddle cinch on Blue and taking care of Millie, Morgan gathered some wood and built a fire. Soon he had a pot of coffee going. For a fall day it had turned out unseasonably warm. Scattered clouds had been passing overhead all day. Morgan noticed that to the northwest there was some dark thunderheads forming. *It'll probably rain again tonight,* he thought to himself. He got a blanket out of the pack and placed it on the ground by a fallen log so Rose could lean back on it and rest a bit. After the coffee was done, they sat back, sipping it for a few minutes and enjoying the serenity of the quiet and peaceful afternoon. After a while, Rose dozed off again. He sat there quietly watching her as she slept. After a while it dawned on him that he was staring at her. He didn't like it, but she was starting to get under his hide. After putting out the fire and cleaning things up, he woke Rose and they started walking down the trail, Blue and Millie following behind them.

"Why have you been so quiet?" she asked, "May I ask what you're thinking?"

"Oh, nothing really." Then changing the subject he pointed to the northwest. "See those clouds over there? In case it rains tonight I'm trying to think of a place we can camp and be out of the weather." But actually, he was forming a plan on how he could draw Whiting out in the open without getting Rose hurt. Mounting Blue again, they rode for a spell, this time Rose riding in the back.

"Like wild raspberries?" he asked as he stopped the horse.

"Sure," she answered. Slipping off, he picked her a handfull thinking it would give her something to do as they rode on.

Topping a little ridge, they found themselves looking down into the Pine River Valley. Easing Blue down the trail, he knew the perfect place he could set up his little surprise for the greedy trio. When reaching the bottom, Morgan put a lead rope on Millie. Swinging back up on Blue, he urged the horses into the stream. Blue carefully picked his way across and Millie reluctantly followed. The crossing wasn't too bad because the water was low.

On the other side, the trail turned up the river and gradually went up along the hillside. After going for about a mile, they turned Blue off the path and into a small park next to the river. It was a peaceful place. There were a few scattered pines and large quakies providing abundant shade. With lots of grass growing down along the river as well as back in the trees, the horses could fill their bellies. It was a perfect place to rest up and relax and get some supper fixed. Here the river made a slight bend to the right as it ran over a natural dam, creating a wide spot of ripples. At the bottom of the ripples the water backwashed into a deep, still pool of water. The water in the pool was a little better than waist deep and a big flat rock jutted out into the water on the right. From the left the grass grew about a foot high along the edge of the water right up to the rock. The river had undercut the dirt at this spot so a person could wade right up to the bank and still be in waist deep water.

Morgan made the horses comfortable so they could graze but he didn't want to unsaddle or unpack them in case they needed to leave quickly. He started a fire and, as usual, put on the coffee pot.

****

Two Bears had been viewing all of this activity from a safe distance downwind of the travelers. He had accomplished this by staying high off the southern ridges and well back in the trees.

Finding a good spot overlooking a large area, he would discreetly hide himself and keep them in view until they moved out of sight. Then he would move on and do the same thing again. He had viewed with interest their encounter with the three white men. What was especially intriguing was the fact that the three had gone down the trail until out of sight and then had turned around and started trailing Morgan and the woman. This concerned Two Bears and he was sure they were up to no good. He would have to be careful not to be seen and, most of all, he didn't want Morgan hurt, or worse, until he could decide for sure what he wanted to do about the situation.

Eleven

Rose walked over to the flat rock jutting out into the water, slipped off her moccasins and rolled up her pant legs. She sat down with her feet in the cool water.

"How's the water?" he asked inquisitively, as he walked up and looked down at her.

"Cool," she replied, not bothering to look up, "but it sure feels good."

"You know what I think I'll do?" he asked, but not giving her a chance to answer, he added, ""I think I'm going swimming since it'll probably be the last chance I'll have this summer."

"You're going to do *what*?" she exclaimed, this time looking up in disbelief at his smiling face.

"I'm going swimming," he said very firmly.

"Are you crazy?" she said, pulling her feet out of the water and standing up. Looking him in the eye, her hands solidly planted on her hips, she added, "It's too cold. You'll freeze to death!"

"No, I won't," he assured her, shaking his head. Then with a big grin on his face, he continued, "I'm a man so I can take it. Nothing to it! Besides it'll get the blood flowing."

"You mean *freeze* the blood, don't you?" She said, laughing as he turned and walked back to where Millie was grazing. Reaching the pack, he turned to Rose.

"Want to join me?"

"No!" was the emphatic answer. "That's one thing you're not getting me to do—go into that cold water!"

"Sissy," he yelled back at her as he started rummaging through the pack. First he took out a clean pair of trousers and a shirt and carefully laid them across a limb growing from the tree next to Millie. Then finding a towel, he carefully reached down in the pack and found his extra Colt 45. He always kept it loaded except for the empty chamber the hammer was on. Quickly and expertly he fixed that problem and it was ready to fire. With his hands still in the pack, he gently wrapped the gun in the towel in a way he hoped would hide it. Returning to where Rose had put her feet back in the water, he laid the towel down hoping she wouldn't see the weapon. Then, walking over to a quakie tree growing nearby, he unbuckled his gunbelt and hung it on a dead branch out in plain sight. Returning once more to the rock, he sat down and started taking off his boots.

"Where's Dawg?" she asked, looking around.

Taking his socks and shirt off and laying his hat on top of them, he stood up and emptied everything out of his pants pockets. "Oh, he's probably scouting the area," he replied, picking up the towel and walking to the edge of the rock.

"I can't believe it. You're really going into that cold water and all this time I thought you were a level-headed person!" She splashed some water towards him with her feet.

"If you weren't such a sissy, you'd come on in and show the world how tough you really are," he dared her.

"Well, sissy or not, tough or not, I'm not going into that water," she said with a note of finality in her voice.

Figuring he had lost the argument, Morgan stepped off into the shallow end of the pool. When the water hit his feet and crept up his legs, it almost took his breath away. *Man, it's cold,* he thought, but he couldn't let Rose know. It had to look like he was having the time of his life.

Forcing a big silly grin on his face, he waded over to the grassy side of the pool facing the fire and laid the towel in the grass. Mustering up all the courage he could, he dove into the pool and it was all he could do to keep from hollering out loud. Coming up from the water, he groped for the towel on the bank. As he reached it and picked it up, the gun slipped out on the ground and was hidden in the grass. Keeping the towel wrapped up like it had been, he dabbed the water off his face and waded a few feet over to the rock and laid it down next to the edge of the grassy bank. Rose was almost hysterical, laughing at him.

"You're freezing to death, aren't you?" she teased.

"Oh, it's a little nippy," he admitted, lowering himself back down in the water and dog-paddling around, trying to keep a straight face. "It's actually very refreshing."

"I'll just bet it is," she said, thoroughly enjoying the situation.

If this was going to work, he hoped they'd hurry up. To be honest, he didn't know how much more he could stand. Just then the dog came trotting up, the hair on his back bristling. *That's a good sign,* Morgan thought as he cupped a handful of water and showered him. Shaking himself, the dog scampered into the brush, out of sight. Grabbing another handful of water, he turned toward Rose.

"Don't you dare," she warned him, covering her face with her hands.

Just then he caught a movement at the fire and, dropping the water, he looked up and saw a rifle aimed right at them. Crazy Bill Whiting was at the other end. Rose let out a cry of alarm.

"Take it easy, Rose. It'll be all right," Morgan assured her softly.

"Well, well, Mr. Morgan, looks like I caught you with your trousers down, so to speak," Whiting said, apparently amused at the predicament that Morgan seemed to be in.

"Ain't funny, Whiting. What do you want?"

"Nothing much. Just fixing to make myself a little money by taking this fine young lady off your hands and returning her to her daddy," Whiting replied as he walked closer to the man and woman at the river bank. "And it looks like you're not in much of a position to do anything about it, as far as I can tell."

"Well, I'm not going anyplace with you!" Rose said, standing and facing him defiantly. "Fletcher won't let you take me anywhere."

Whiting laughed again. "It doesn't look like your hero is going to do anything except turn blue. Is that water *cold*, Morgan?" Then, raising his voice, he called, "Come on in boys, and bring the horses with you."

Soon the Banks brothers came out of the trees leading their horses. Tying them up to some quakies, they came over and stood by Whiting. Charlie grinned, exposing his missing tooth as he said, "Howdy, ma'am." Tom just glared at the shivering man standing in the water.

"Here, Charlie, take the rifle and keep it aimed at Mr. Morgan," Whiting said, as he handed the gun to the older Banks brother. "Make sure he doesn't try anything stupid."

After handing the gun to Charlie, Whiting started toward Rose. Stopping at the quakie, he lifted Morgan's gun belt off the limb and motioned for Rose to come over. As she approached, he instructed her.

"You, young lady, can fix me and the boys some grub. We haven't eaten all day and I'm starved!"

"I'm not fixing you anything! If you want to eat, fix it yourself!" Rose exclaimed.

Whiting stopped and started toward her, raising his arm as if he was going to slap her. Then Morgan spoke up.

"Whiting, there's no need to hurt her. Please, Rose, do as he says. I don't want you getting hurt. It's just not worth it."

"Now that's plumb neighborly of you, Morgan," Whiting mockingly retorted. "You're talking sense now." Turning back to Rose, he continued, "And, Missy, you'd better listen to him and save yourself some grief."

Tom Banks was back at the fire pouring himself a cup of coffee.

"Pour me one, too, little brother," Charlie piped up. Tom walked over and handed Charlie his cup and headed back to get him another one.

"What happens now?" Morgan inquired.

"Well, I guess there's no harm in telling you," Whiting mused, taking his turn at the coffee pot. "First, we're going to have some supper and then we'll decide what to do with *you*. We'll probably have to tie the woman up so she doesn't wander off. After a good night's rest, we'll head back and soon she'll be in the arms of her daddy and the reward will be in our pockets."

"My father will never pay you a dime!" Rose said, coming back to the fire with some things to fix for supper. "I won't let him."

"Oh, he'll pay us one way or the other and if he doesn't, he'll never see his little girl alive again. In fact, I think we'll ask double the going price." Pausing, he smiled an evil smile. "Oh, he'll pay, all right!"

"And what are you going to do with Fletcher?" she asked, standing up in Whiting's face. "You'd better not hurt him!"

"Lady, you're scaring me to death," Whiting said, displaying a smirk on his face. "But it is a good question. We could just leave him here without a horse or gun, but if he survived, he'd hunt us down. Ever last one of us, that's for sure. And I don't think I want to spend the rest of my life looking over my shoulder all the time. On the other hand, it's probably best just to let Tom here put him out of his misery and that way we won't have to be worrying about him hunting us down." For the first time, Morgan saw Tom Banks smile.

"Are you going to shoot me while I'm standing in this water or are you going to let me get out before I freeze to death?" Morgan asked, edging toward the towel. "That wouldn't give your blood-thirsty friend his thrill, now would it?"

Just as Morgan was about to touch the towel, Whiting yelled at him. "Don't touch it! Move back away from it right now! Do you think I'm stupid or something? I had a feeling this was too easy. You think you've set us up, don't you?" He paused before continuing on. "I didn't think it was this easy to get the drop on Fletcher Morgan. You have a gun in that towel, don't you?"

"Okay, okay, you're wise to me, I underestimated you," Morgan said as he moved back away from the towel. With his hand dragging along the grassy bank, he gradually came closer and closer to the hidden six-gun.

"I won't let you hurt him," Rose said angrily, as she went for Whiting with the frying pan she had in her hand. "And if you do, I'll see that you are hunted down and hanged."

Grabbing her by the wrists, he wrenched the pan out of her grasp and it fell to the ground. "Shut up and fix the food," he snapped. "You can't do anything to stop us and if you don't keep quiet, we'll deliver a dead body to your father. In any case, he'll pay us."

"Well, you can murder me then, but I'm not fixing you scums anything to eat," she said as she sat down on the log and folded her arms. She was surprised she was standing up to the bully that way.

"Oh, get out of the way! I'll fix it myself," bellowed Whiting.

Maybe this was the distraction Morgan was waiting for. He had found the revolver and closed his hand tightly around the grip. Very slowly he put his thumb on the hammer and quietly cocked the gun. He was ready for the right opportunity. Charlie was still holding the rifle in his general direction and Tom was leaning on the trunk of a big pine tree drinking his coffee with his left hand. *That's a break,* Morgan thought. Whiting had his back turned to Morgan, fooling with the fire. Rose was sitting on the log to the right of the fire, crying. Out of the corner of his eye, Morgan caught a glimpse of the dog sneaking up behind Tom Banks. It was time to act before Whiting saw the dog.

"Get 'em, Dawg," Morgan yelled as he raised his gun and fired a round into the shoulder of Charlie Banks. Instantly the dog lunged at Tom Banks, grabbing his left wrist with a death-like grip and holding on with all his might. Tom let out a yell, trying to shake the dog off. Charlie was lying flat on the ground, the shock of the bullet had almost knocked him cold.

Whiting, who had been turned towards the fire when the ruckus started, dropped the frying pan and grabbed for his gun. Then he heard Morgan's warning. "Don't go for it, Bill or I'll drop you in your tracks!" With his back still to Morgan, Whiting was motionless, trying to decide if he should turn and draw against the man standing in the water. "I mean it, Bill!" Morgan warned again. "You touch that gun and you are a dead man."

"Okay, take it easy," Whiting said as he slowly raised his hands and turned around.

The dog still had a hold on Tom, even though he was jumping up and down and beating the dog with his free hand. "Call off this damn dog," he cried out in pain.

"Okay, Dawg, let the poor man loose," Morgan said, as the dog reluctantly released his grip on Tom Banks' bleeding arm. Poor Charlie was sitting up now, shaking his head and trying to clear it as he held his bleeding shoulder with his left hand. "All right, everyone, stand real still and don't even think of moving, because I'm very cold and a little annoyed, so don't rile me any further," he warned the defeated trio. Speaking to Tom, leaning on the tree and holding his shredded arm, he ordered, "You, take your gun out of its holster with your good hand and carefully lay it on the ground and get over by the fire." The hurting man promptly obeyed. "Whiting, throw your weapon down, too, and while you're at it, get the gun and knife off Charlie and put it with yours." Whiting carefully took his gun out and laid it on the ground. Walking over to Charlie, he relieved him of his weapons and laid them down beside his own. "And," Morgan added, "you might as well get the hidden knife off Tom and lay it by the guns."

"What knife?" he asked innocently.

"You know what knife," Morgan snapped, "now *get it*!"

Reluctantly, Whiting took the knife out of Tom's left boot and tossed it on the ground.

"Rose, would you please gather up their weapons and put them over by Millie for me?" Morgan asked as he started to ease toward the rock. Rose, who had not said anything since the ruckus started, hurried and gathered up the guns and knives and laid them by the tree Millie was tied to.

Pulling himself out of the water, he picked up the towel with his free hand and proceeded to dry himself. Once that was done, he hobbled over to the trio in his bare feet. Motioning with his gun, he ordered the three of them to get over by the log Rose had been sitting on.

"Tom, sit down. Bill, help Charlie over there so he can sit down, too. Then you had better look after their wounds before one of them bleeds to death."

It turned out that Charlie wasn't hurt bad since the bullet had gone clean through his shoulder and hadn't even hit a bone. Though he was in quite a bit of pain, he would live. Tom Banks' arm was torn up pretty bad and there was quite a bit of bleeding. Morgan asked Rose to bring some water from the river and then told Whiting to clean and wrap their wounds.

"While you boys are busy with that, I think I'm going to change into some dry clothes. Dawg, you watch them and if they start anything, eat 'em alive." Without turning to Rose, he warned her not to stand where she would be in the line of fire, in case they decided to do something foolish while he was changing.

Going over behind the pack on Millie's back, he could change and at the same time keep an eye on the three desperados. After he got into some dry clothes and Rose had brought him his boots, he strapped his gunbelt back on.

"Man, I feel a hundred percent better. I thought I was going to freeze to death before you fellows showed up. But now we can have some coffee and decide what to do with you three naughty boys."

"I *knew* it! You were waiting for us," Whiting stammered. "You set us up and lured us right into a trap like a bunch of dummies!"

"I didn't set you up," Morgan said, shaking his head. "Your greed did. I figured you thought there was some easy money to be had, only I wanted you to try to get it on my terms and not yours. Lucky for us, that's exactly what you did."

Looking up at the sun, Morgan figured it must be three o'clock by now. They would need to hurry if they were to get to the place he had planned on spending the night. The storm clouds were still building up and there was little doubt that it would be pouring before the night was over. Bill Whiting had dressed the wounds of the two Banks brothers, but they were hurting quite a bit. All three were sitting on the log smarting from their humiliation. Morgan stood before the three of them.

"Tell you fellows what we're going to do." He paused, then began again. "Maybe I should just put a bullet in each of you, just like you were going to do to me, and leave your bodies to rot out here." Turning towards the woman, he asked, "Rose, would you want me to do that?"

"No," she replied softly, "I wouldn't."

"That's what I figured. See guys? She saved your miserable lives, but I guess I feel the same way, even though I can hardly stomach the three of you. I think I'll give you a chance to get out of this mess alive. So here's what we're going to do. We're going to take your guns, boots, and horses..."

"Wait a minute!" Whiting piped up. "That's giving us a death sentence. Being out here unarmed, on foot and barefooted to boot, that's just plain murder. You have a *big* heart, Morgan," he said sarcastically.

"You thought nothing of murdering me, you scum," Morgan snapped back, "but let me finish, will you? After we leave, we'll put your guns alongside the trail up there by the curve." He pointed to a spot up the trail. "We'll leave your boots and horses up where Coon Creek comes into the river. You know where that is?"

"Yeah, I know, but that's a long way to go in bare feet," Whiting protested.

"Well, that's tough, but that's what happens when little men get greedy. Now stop whining and take your medicine. At least you're still alive."

Tom Banks looked up at Morgan with an icy stare. "We'll meet again someday, you, me, and that dog, so you better kill me now while you have the chance."

"Now pay attention, all three of you," Morgan said in a tone that left no doubt as to the seriousness of his next words. "First of all, I'm going to report you to the proper authorities when we get to town, including the Army. Secondly, Rose will probably tell her father and two brothers what you did and, more importantly, what you were planning to do. From what she tells me, I wouldn't want to be in this neck of the woods and take a chance on them finding me. They have a lot of friends, too. So think hard before you stick around." Catching his breath, he got dead serious. "Now personally, I'm going to tell you this. If you follow or try to even up the score or if I ever see you again, I'm going to kill you without hesitation. Do you understand me? Whiting, you better tell these two that I mean what I say. Do you understand?"

"We understand," Whiting grumbled under his breath.

"Let's get out of here," Morgan said to Rose as he turned and started picking things up and putting them in Millie's pack. He soon had everything ready to go. "Okay, boys, off with the boots and hurry up or I'll sic the dog on you."

"Okay, okay," muttered Whiting, as he took off his boots and helped the brothers with theirs. Morgan took the boots and tied them across the saddles of their horses and, taking their gunbelts, he hung them from their saddle horns.

"Rose, you ride Blue," he said, helping her up. Then he addressed the trio on the log. "Boys, I want you all to sit there on the log until we get to the curve and to make sure you do, the dog is staying until we get there." Swinging up on one of their horses, he told the dog, "Watch them, boy, until I whistle. Don't let them move an inch."

With that, they started out. Morgan took the lead, the other two horses behind him. Rose and Blue came next with Millie bringing up the rear. When they reached the curve in the trail, they stopped and Morgan tossed the gun belts off the side of the trail a few feet.

"This will give us time to get up the trail a piece. It won't take them long to get here and they'll have some protection."

"Leave their boots too, please," Rose turned to him with a pleading look.

"You have a soft heart, don't you?" he said, grinning at her.

"I don't know, I guess I do," she replied. "I just feel sorry for them now."

"Okay, you win," he said. "It will be dark soon and that will slow them down. Besides, I don't think they have nerve enough to follow us anyway. They're going to have to find a place that's dry or they're going to get a good soaking and that oughta keep them busy for awhile." Untying the boots, he tossed them by the guns. Turning in his saddle, he let out a loud whistle and started down the trail again. They had only gone a little ways when the dog caught up with them. *I wonder if he chewed them up a little,* Morgan mused to himself.

It wasn't long until they came to Coon Creek. Stopping, Morgan led their horses off the trail into some quakies and tied them securely. He took the saddles off and dragged them into some brush so they would have to look for them. He wanted to buy as much time as he could so they could get a good head start. It wouldn't be too long until dark and the cloud cover was moving in fast now. It was sure to start raining soon and he needed to reach the camping place he had in mind. They would be good and dry there.

"Are you getting tired?" he asked her.

"Yes," she replied, "it's been a busy day. I'm exhausted."

"We're going to get off this trail and head for a cave I know of. We'll have a dry place to eat and sleep and we both need the rest. Just hang in there for a little while longer."

****

Two Bears had watched the unfolding drama with great interest and amusement. He had circled high on the ridge, keeping well out of sight. He was careful to keep on the downwind side of the dog because he had no desire to hurt the animal, but if the dog came for him again, he would kill him. It had worked out well for him since the breeze was coming from the northwest, allowing him to creep

up fairly close to the camp from the southwest. He was on the opposite side of the river from the confrontation, lying in the tall grass with a clear view of the proceedings. As he laid there watching, he figured the dumb white man had been foolish and left himself open to being taken. The Indian had wanted to stay hidden, but he couldn't let the woman get hurt. He decided to deal himself in. In fact, he had rested his rifle on the ground in front of him and, taking careful aim on Charlie Banks, he was just about to pull the trigger when Morgan fired.
 Again he had underestimated the white man. He was starting to see him in a new light. His grandfather was right—he was an honorable man. If Two Bears was in the white man's shoes, he would have killed all three of the evil men, yet he had let them live. His growing respect for him as a worthy enemy was starting to affect the way he was going to deal with his dilemma.

Twelve

Turning Blue up Coon Creek, they started working their way up the hillside. They soon topped out and had to pick their way along the edge of a deep, wide canyon. Lightning was beginning to flash along the horizon and Morgan could see the storm working its way down from the northwest. It wasn't long before they came to a tiny stream that was fed by springs near the top of the ridge. Just north of it, maybe a hundred feet, was an outcropping of rocks that formed a good sized indentation that would provide suitable protection from the weather and the night.

"Will this do?" he said to the woman sitting in front of him.

"Looks great to me," she replied, relieved that they were finally stopping for the night.

After dismounting and helping Rose off, he tied the horses securely to a dead piñon tree that had fallen near their chosen camp. The broken limbs would make it easy to gather the nightly supply of wood. It wasn't long before he had piled up a considerable amount for the night. As he went about taking care of the horses, Rose gathered up some stones and built a place for a fire and, after a couple of tries, had a small one going. As Morgan unpacked Millie, he carried the packs to the back of the shelter. Rose, by this time, had caught on to camp cooking and had started their meal. Unsaddling Blue, Morgan led both horses to a nice, grassy spot and staked them out to graze. It had just started to sprinkle by the time he was through. He had just gotten inside when it started raining in earnest, but the two horses didn't seem to mind the refreshing shower, ignoring it as they continued to fill their bellies. Rose had the coffee going and the meal pretty well along by the time Morgan had finished with all the chores.

"Here, let me finish. You need to sit and rest."

"Thank you," she said, yawning. "I *am* tired." Wrapping herself in a blanket and leaning back against the saddle, she dozed off.

Morgan let her sleep awhile before waking her to eat. It was raining hard now and the dog came in, soaking wet, and laid down by the fire. Morgan fixed him up with some biscuits and gravy and afterwards handed Rose her plate. The three ate in silence. After finishing, Morgan took the plates, setting them out in the rain.

"Let's let old Mother Nature do the dishes tonight," he said as he poured a cup of coffee and settled back against a rock. "You sure have been quiet this evening. Has the day been too much for you?"

"It's been a long day, all right," she answered. "It started out so beautiful and I thought that everything was all right and then everything went wrong. I thought they were going to kill you and I didn't know what was going to happen to me. First I wanted you to kill them and then, seeing them hurting and realizing we were safe, I began to feel sorry for them. I've always been protected from those sort of things. I guess I've been shielded from a lot of the realities of life. It's hard to get used to."

"I know," he said, remembering how he felt when he was cast out in the cold world—the rotten people and their attitudes that he had run up against when he had begun to search for his parents' killers. "When I was out on my own," he continued, "I had a hard time accepting some of the things I saw and heard, but, in time, you become calloused and coping with it becomes easier and easier. The scary thing is that if you're not careful, you become just like them." In his heart he hoped she would always stay sensitive, especially of the feelings of others. "You're really homesick now, aren't you?" he asked sympathetically.

Looking at the ground for a few minutes and taking a sip from her cup, she looked back up and their eyes met in the flickering firelight. He saw sadness in them this night, the usual childlike sparkle gone. "Yes, I am. Seems more so tonight. I really miss my home and family or maybe it's the feeling of being safe and sound, the feeling of security that comes from being surrounded by ones you love and who love you. Maybe it's like throwing the covers over your head at night and feeling safe by doing it." She paused. "Don't take me wrong, Fletcher because I *do* feel safe with you. You've protected me, fed me, cared for me, and I have grown very fond of you and the animals. There are no words I know that can express my appreciation for all you've done and, all kidding aside, I do love your home, the mountains. But it's not the same. I need the kind of home I was raised in—a house, a yard, a garden and outbuildings, you know, like the barn and tool shed. I need family and friends that I can visit with and enjoy good times with. I guess what I'm trying to say is that I need to be rooted in a stable home life." She stopped for a minute, a wistful, far-away look in her eyes. When Morgan didn't say anything, she continued. "Someday, I would like very much to come back to the place that was my home for these past few weeks and visit. To be able to remember and relive the experience I've had, although I could never find it on my own." She paused. "Would you bring me back some day, Fletcher?"

"Anytime you want to, just let me know," he answered, "and that's a promise." The rain had let up. Laying down his cup and getting up, Morgan slipped into his slicker. "I need to check the horses. I'll be right back," he said as he moved out into the darkness.

Rose could hear him moving and talking to the animals and soon he returned, groaning some as he bent over and poured himself a last cup of coffee for the night, offering Rose more as well. She shook her head, saying something about not being able to sleep if she had anymore.

"Man, I'm stiff tonight, and standing in that cold water so long didn't do me much good."

"I can't believe the things you'll do to keep the situation in hand," she said, yawning.

"Being stiff and sore is better than being dead, and I'll go to any lengths to prevent that." Her yawn was a reminder that it was late and she was tired. "Rose, I've been thinking that it would be a good idea for us to rest here tomorrow. I know it will put us a day later getting home, but I think it's best. Would you mind?"

"No, I don't mind at all. I was hoping you would think of something, like letting the horses rest," she said with a wink. "Seriously, I'm anxious to get home, but I'm so tired tonight that I really think it would be best to rest tomorrow."

"Then it's settled. We'll stay here tomorrow and leave the next day. I hope it's not as exciting as today was!"

"Amen to that," she agreed, yawning again.

"The grass is too wet to make you a mattress tonight, so you'll have to rough it and sleep on the cold hard ground. Maybe you've toughened up enough so you can get a decent night's sleep."

Morgan tossed a couple of good-sized logs on the fire as it was turning a little chilly. The rain had started up again, only not as hard this time. He loved sleeping when it rained, lying there and listening to the raindrops hitting the trees and hearing it running off the rocks that sheltered them. As they settled down for the night, the dog crept over and took his customary place at the foot of the woman's bedroll.

The next thing Morgan felt was the sunshine hitting his face. Opening his eyes, he could see that it was late. But it wasn't the sunshine that had woke him. It was the gunfire that had broken the early morning silence. The dreaded sounds came bouncing off the canyon walls, echoing off into the far distance. He could tell they were not too close, maybe down in the river bottom. He thought he heard about half a dozen, but couldn't be sure. There had been a rifle while the others sounded like handguns. What was going on? Did he have something new to worry about? He would have to play it be ear. "We'll have to keep a sharp eye out for trouble," he muttered in annoyance.

He hadn't realized he had been so tired and sore. As he tried to move, he ached all over but when he stood up and stretched, he got his arms and legs where they functioned fairly well again. Picking up some wood, he threw it on the smoldering ashes of last night's fire. He glanced over to see if Rose was still sleeping. The dog was gone so it was for sure he had heard the gunfire. If there was anyone near, the dog would find them. Picking up the coffee pot and walking down to the stream, he splashed water on his face and that brought him abruptly back to life. Taking the pot back to the fire, he got the morning coffee on. That done, he went out and dried and brushed down the horses. Morgan was still concerned about the gunfire. The dog returned and, finding a place on the trail where he could see the canyon below, ears and nose pointed to the southwest, he started his watch. *Wonder what he knows,* Morgan thought as he turned towards the camp.

Getting a fresh cup of coffee, Morgan found a good-sized rock overlooking their back trail. He could see where they had come up the side of the hill and also the canyon bottoms that ran both east and west of the little ridge their trail was on. Scooting back under a deformed Juniper tree and finding a comfortable spot, he spent the rest of the morning watching for anyone following them as he drank coffee and thought about the events of the past few weeks. After the rain, the ground had a fresh, earthy smell and everything looked clean and new from nature's bath of the night before. The sky was almost completely clear and the warm autumn sun was once again warming and drying the paradise he called home.

Although he felt an occasional gust of the morning breeze brush against his face, he was oblivious of the noise it made playing in the trees and hardly noticed a bluejay chattering at a ground squirrel busily gathering acorns for his winter food supply. His cup had been empty for some time. Leaving the dog to watch, he walked back to the pot, not able to shake the gut feeling that he had come to a fork in this road of life once more. He was going to have to make a decision on which direction his life was going to take. Just when he thought he had life figured out, it threw him a curve and now he was confused again.

By the look of the sun, it was close to noon. As he reached the cook fire, Rose was just beginning to stir. By the time he had fixed something to eat, she was up and had downed a hot cup of coffee. While they were eating Morgan started the conversation.

"Rose, while you were sleeping this morning, I was sitting out yonder on a rock and doing some thinking. To tell you the truth, I haven't done this much thinking in *years*!"

"Can I ask what you were thinking about?" she inquired politely.

"What's been going over and over in my mind is what you've said about having a home. Belonging somewhere special and leaving something to be remembered by."

"What are you trying to say?" she asked, her curiosity aroused.

"Just this. I was offered a little spread up one of the canyons that runs into the Florida River, just northeast of Durango. You remember me telling you about my friend in the Army?"

"Yes, I remember. You would go home with him at times and, if I remember right, you've spent the last few winters at his folks' place."

"That's right. Well, early last summer I dropped by to see them and help around the place for a few days. While I was there, they told me of their plans to sell out and move into Animas City. She has a sister living there and a little house next to hers is up for sale by the bank. The house will be available the first of October. If they can, they want to move into town before winter sets in." He paused and cleared his throat. "Anyway, they offered their ranch to me. They said they wanted me to have it and make it my home and that they would wait until the first of October for me to make up my mind. If they don't hear from me, then they'll have to accept the offer made by a rancher living just to the west of them."

"What have you decided?" she asked, excitement in her voice.

"That's the problem. I can't decide," he replied, shaking his head. 'Being out in the mountains this summer, I thought I had made up my mind. Then I met you and you got me thinking about a home and now I just don't know. I'm confused as to what I want to do with the rest of my life."

"Excuse me for asking and maybe it's none of my business, but is it the money? I mean, do you have enough money to buy a place like that?" She turned a light shade of red, embarrassed that she had been so nosy. "Forgive me. I know it's not my business."

"No, that's all right. Money's not the problem," he said thoughtfully. "I still have most of the money left me by my parents. I've saved most of my earnings all these years and I find a bit of gold each summer, more than I've needed to live on. Besides, they only want half the selling price now and then a payment each year until it's paid for or until their deaths, whichever comes first. If they die before I have paid them in full, the rest of the debt would be canceled. No," he repeated, "the money is not the problem."

"I know what the problem is," she said with a silly little grin on her face and a childish sparkle in the green eyes.

"Oh, you do, do you?" Returning her grin and looking straight into her eye, he challenged her. "Okay, what is it?"

"You just don't want to give up your freedom."

"My freedom? What on earth are you talking about?"

"I mean your *freedom*! Freedom to roam around these mountains. Freedom to come and go whenever and wherever you want to. The freedom that is afforded you by not being responsible for anyone else, except maybe your animal friends. Out here you're protected from getting close to anyone and being responsible for anyone...you don't have to answer to any man..or woman. That's the freedom I'm talking about."

"I just don't know," he said, looking at the ground and shaking his head. He reached for the coffee pot and poured himself another cup. "Maybe you're right. That's what the old man told me, too. I can just picture him saying, 'Son, it's time you settled down and built something for yourself. Stop this foolish roaming around the country. You'll end up a bum.' Maybe it *is* time to do that." He stirred the fire with a stick, deep in thought. "Trouble is, I *do* love these mountains and I *do* love the freedom my life affords me. To see what's over the next ridge or range, following a river to see where it comes from and where it goes. To be able to stop and pan for gold or fish for as long as I please. It's true that I like not being accountable to anyone but myself. I try hard not to hurt anyone unless they give me no choice."

"Fletcher," her voice was gentle as she spoke, "are you afraid that you may get close to someone and then lose them—like you did your parents?"

The question set him back a bit. Was that the real reason he had always taken special pains to make sure he didn't get close to anyone? Was this lady seeing in him something he had refused to acknowledge himself?"

"I don't know what to say to that," he admitted.

"It's true you lost your parents and your good friend, whom you were evidently very close to. But you didn't lose your brother and surely there's other people that you have been fond of that are still living, so you needn't fear getting close to others who will come into your life. I hope I have become your friend and I'm not going to die, at least not while *you're* around!" She gently touched his arm and then thought it best to change the subject. "Your way of life does have its advantages, I can't argue with that," she conceded, "but I also think it has some major disadvantages." Without thinking, she returned to the touchy subject. "For instance, a person needs to share their life with someone they care for. Someone they can get close to and trust. It's very satisfying to care for someone and be cared for. There's a lot to say about giving of oneself. By giving, you receive many times over." They sat silently for awhile and she could tell he was thinking about what she had said. Finally she asked him, "Have I been a burden to you?"

Looking up in surprise at the unexpected question, he blurted out, "*No!*" Then, slightly embarrassed by his response, he added somewhat sheepishly, "Not at all. I've enjoyed the time you've been with me. It's been a unique experience, though I'm sorry your family has had to suffer, not knowing that you're safe. But I wouldn't trade the last few weeks for anything in the world." Grinning, he added, "In fact, I might even be willing to give your *father* a thousand dollars for the time you've been with me!"

"Thank you for that thought," she said, blushing. "By the way, what are you going to do with your reward money?"

"Not accept it, for one thing. Nobody should have to be paid for helping another person in trouble but, if he insists, I'll just give it to you. For *sure*, I won't take it!"

"I knew that's what you'd say. I just *knew* it!"

They spent the rest of the day resting and watching from the rim rock for any signs of being followed, and they took a walk along the canyon rim later in the afternoon. There wasn't much conversation. They both seemed to have a few things they were mulling over in their minds. The only life stirring were a few deer. They stopped and watched them work their way up the opposite side of the canyon. Later, after supper when the necessary chores were done, they sat contentedly by the fire. Rose did most of the talking. Morgan just listened as she filled him in about her flowers and things around the house she enjoyed doing. He built up the fire and suggested that they turn in early, as they had a long day ahead of them.

Though he spent most of the night lying in his bedroll thinking, he got up early the next morning. There was a skim of frost on the ground, but it wouldn't last long as the sun peaked over the mountain tops. He started the day by packing most of the gear, except what they would need for breakfast. As usual, he fixed biscuits and gravy. He fed the dog and ate himself, setting a plate aside for Rose. He decided to let her sleep as long as he could. Coming back to the fire after getting the horses ready, he woke her and finished packing while she ate.

It was between eight and nine o'clock by the time they were ready to leave. The dog had been out since before daylight and when he returned he seemed content that everything was under control. It was a beautiful day, the sky was clear except for a few scattered clouds. The sun was bathing the earth with its warmth and there was a refreshing breeze blowing from the southwest.

"This is going to be a good day," Morgan said as he headed Blue out along the canyon rim.

"I feel good today, too, " Rose commented, "although I'm still a little stiff. I'm glad I slept well last night."

"See, you're getting hardened for this kind of life," Morgan kidded her.

"Well, I may have become a hardened mountain lady, but it's going to be oh so nice to sleep in my soft, warm feather bed again. And before you say anything, I do admit I'm going to miss this experience."

"I guess we can take it easy on you this final leg of the journey. We can't make Durango today anyway, so we'll stop at the Florida River this afternoon and have a final trout dinner. We'll go in tomorrow."

"What time tomorrow will we get there?" she asked with a bit of anxiety in her voice.

"Even taking it easy, we should reach town in the late afternoon," was his answer.

The trail started dropping off the ridge and was winding itself out of the pines and down alongside a huge mountain meadow. Along the sides of the clearing was a large quakie grove. The trail followed alongside these for a considerable distance. The quakies were sparsely spaced, allowing a lot of light in and the grass was growing abundantly—it was knee-high to a horse. They were quiet as they rode, with only an occasional snort from Blue or Millie to break the quiet of the day. The quakies already had a good start on changing from the pale green of summer to their deep yellow fall colors. A slight breeze seemed to play a song as it passed through the leaves, causing them to rustle. Now and then one would break free from its branch and float in a twirling motion as it gently fell to the ground.

Suddenly the horses raised their heads and looked to the left, their ears straight up, straining to hear as two timberline buck deer came out of the oak brush behind the quakies. Turning parallel to the horses, they walked beside the group as if they were just as curious of the humans as the humans were of them.

"Look at that!" Morgan said, pointing.

Rose, turning a bit to the side, was awed by the beauty of the pair. The biggest was the grandfather of all deer and the one following him was a big buck, too, but was dwarfed by the size and grandeur of the older one. Holding their heads high and their ears pointed forward, they pranced alongside for quite a spell. Finally, as the trail veered off to the right and the quakies gave way to a large meadow, the deer bounced away, their white tails the last thing to be seen as they disappeared over the mountain's edge.

"That was beautiful," Rose said, as they disappeared. "I've never seen deer so close or so big. It was breathtaking."

"That's the kind of thing a person sees up here all the time," he responded proudly. "You can see deer, elk, bear, and all kinds of little critters and birds. You can hear the songs of the wind blowing through the trees...each kind of tree has a different song. You can hear the music of the water in the streams as it tumbles over the rocks or enjoy the roar of the waterfall. Then there's the serenity of the small mountain lakes as the water laps the shore. I could go on all day long talking about what it's like to live here. Really, Rose, the mountains are a special place. I would really miss them."

"I know you would," she admitted. "As I've said before, you go together, you and the mountains."

They had been riding for some time now and had just reached an area cleared by a wildfire in the not-so-distant past. There wasn't much standing except for the ghost-like blackened stakes that were at one time a hearty stand of spruce. Some grass and a few ground plants had started to grow, giving it a speckled appearance. It was a grand example of nature renewing itself. The trail was wider and ran fairly level for a considerable distance so, stopping and dismounting, Morgan suggested that they stretch their legs and walk a bit. Rose thought it a good idea and they started down the path side by side. She was curious about the fire and Morgan attempted to explain how nature renews the vegetation from time to time. Rose could sense that his mind was somewhere else, so she was content to walk in silence and leave this mountain man to his thoughts.

The Rescue of Fletcher Morgan

Thirteen

Morgan had two things that were weighing on his mind. First, he couldn't help worrying about the gunfire two days ago. The dog seemed a bit nervous also and he was always stopping and staring towards the south. If they were being followed, then who was it? He didn't think Bill Whiting and his buddies would have the guts. The only other possibility would be Two Bears and how would *he* know where they were? Out of the blue, Rose spoke.

"It would be hard for you to settle down and be tied to one place, wouldn't it?" There wasn't an immediate answer and she wondered if she really wanted to hear his response. After a thoughtful pause he finally answered.

"I don't know. I honestly don't know."

"What if you had a ranch in the mountains?" she asked.

He pondered the question for a few minutes. "That has possibilities, I suppose."

"The place you mentioned yesterday, it's in the mountains, isn't it? Please tell me about it."

"Well, it's not in the high country. In fact, it's at a lower elevation than we're at right now, but it reminds me in many ways of the mountains in general. I suppose a man could take a trip to the high country now and then and do a little hunting and prospecting."

"I would love to hear about it—the ranch, I mean," she said, trying not to sound too eager.

"Let's see, there's about three sections of land and there's a large valley that runs almost due north and south that practically splits the ranch in half. A small stream runs the full length of it and eventually empties into the river. The place has several good-sized meadows that would be good for grazing or maybe putting up feed for the winter. Lots of timber and most of the hillsides have a southern exposure, providing lots of sunshine in the winter."

"The house. What about the house?" she interrupted, anxious to hear about it.

"It sits on the southern end of the ranch. In fact, it's in the mouth of the valley I was just mentioning. The stream passes on the east side and on the west there's a sloping hill that has pine trees growing all over the top. On top of this hill you can see the house, all the out-buildings, and almost clear to the river."

"The house?" she said again, impatiently.

"It's not much now because it needs to be completed. There's a kitchen and living area in one room and the other room is a bedroom. The house faces south with a covered porch in front. You can sit on that porch and watch the sun come up and watch it go down without moving if you want to. It was built with logs, making it warm in the winter and cool in the summer. Mrs. Olsen makes it feel homey, if you know what I mean."

"I know," she replied. "That's how our home is. Where does the Mexican family live?"

"Olsen had a two-room shack built for them, oh, three maybe four hundred yards to the north, down along the stream. There's a half-finished tool shed not far from it and then to the west is a partially built barn. Olsen had really bought the land for his son and was saving it for him, for when he got a belly-full of being a soldier. When George died, he sort of give up on it. The place really needs a lot of work."

"Well, you're young and strong. You could do it!" she assured him.

"Think so?" He laughed.

"I know so," she teased back, "and just think, you'd have a real home that you could call your own."

Morgan didn't comment, but it was something that was weighing heavily on his mind. By now they had walked for some time and had come to a point on the trail where they could see for miles in several directions. Sitting down on the up-hill side of the path, Morgan motioned Rose to join him.

"We'll stop and rest up a bit," he said, "and admire the scenery for a spell."

"It's lovely," she said, "so peaceful and warm right here. I'm tempted to take a short nap." Lying back, she folded her arms behind her neck and closed her eyes. "Do you mind?"

"Not at all," he said. "Be my guest."

He'd let her sleep for half an hour or so. As he leaned back on one elbow, his body drank in the warmth of the noon-day sun. But he was unaware of his surroundings as he stared off at the distant peaks, lost in his thoughts of the future and what might be in it for him. Startled by the stirring of the dog, he woke up from his trance. Turning, he fixed his gaze on the peacefully sleeping woman. She was a treasure, he thought, far more precious than all the gold or silver in his beloved mountains. Her delicate frailness made her even more attractive to him. She had a softness and gentleness that he had never felt in the wilds of his wilderness. Could he have them both? Was it right to have them both? Why, oh *why*, did life have to be so complicated?

Time was getting away and they needed to move on, so he woke her. Breaking out some left-over biscuits from breakfast, along with a couple pieces of jerky, he handed her some.

"Let's eat on the way," he said. He was getting anxious to get to the river and set up camp for the night.

As they came down off a ridge and broke through a stand of spruce, they found themselves in a small clearing surrounded by a mixture of quakies and a few scattered pines. Near the center was a little pond created by a stream and a busy beaver. Morgan started laughing and, of course, she wanted to know what was so funny.

"This clearing brought back a memory of something funny that happened a few years ago. I almost died laughing, but one person in our party didn't think it was so funny at the time."

"Well, are you going to tell me so I can share your memory?" she wanted to know.

"If you want to hear about it, why not? It all happened when George and I, with a couple of other men we knew, took a trip back up in the high country. Our destination was up near the Continental Divide, north of Pagosa Springs. Our objective was to find a cache of gold that supposedly was stashed in a cave by a group of miners. During the summer, according to the story, these miners would bring their gold ore down and put it in this cave and then in the fall they would take it on down to the smelter. They had been having trouble with the Utes and finally the Utes won out and killed them all before they could get the gold moved from the cave down to Pagosa. Anyway, we thought it would be fun to try and put all the stories together and see if we could find it.

"We got to the area where we thought it might be, set up camp by a little lake and got ready to start our search. The next morning we got an early start and as we came off the hillside close to our camp, we saw a herd of elk wandering through the spruce trees below us. We decided to follow them and see how close we could get. I saw some going through the trees on my right and started to follow, but all I could see was a glimpse of one every now and then. We came to this little clearing and standing in the middle of it was a young cow and she turned and was looking at my horse and me. I started towards her, sitting very still in the saddle, and the horse walked very slowly and steadily towards her. We stopped about ten feet from her and just stared at each other for a few minutes. Then she took off.

"As I turned the horse to go back, he decided it was time to take a drink, so we headed for this water hole at the edge of the clearing. This pool of water was about twenty feet across and almost perfectly round. As the horse approached the edge, I could feel the ground give under our weight, it felt kind of spongy. Anyway he stood on the edge and lowered his head and was drinking. About then, George rode up on his horse that he called *Knothead*. Old Knothead wanted a drink, too, but when he got to the edge of the water, he plops both front legs right into the water and, of course, there's no bottom. Well, George and Knothead did a somersault right into the middle of the pool. The top of the water was covered with some kind of water plant, moss or something like that, with little white flowers all over them. George came sputtering to the surface covered from head to foot with this white, flowered, mossy growth. He got to the edge and we pulled him out. He said they didn't even touch bottom when they went in. We never did know how deep it was, but the sides had been undercut by the water and that's why it felt spongy when we rode up to the edge.

"The horse was swimming around and trying to get out, but he couldn't get his front legs up on the bank. He was even trying to lunge at the bank to get out but he couldn't make it. We could see that he was getting tired and we were fixing to throw a rope to him to pull him out, when he made one last desperate jump and got his front legs on solid ground. We grabbed the bridle and helped him pull himself out. It was some sight, the man and his horse standing there soaking wet with this green and white mossy stuff hanging all over them. Soon as we saw that they were all right, we had a good laugh. In fact, we laughed about that little episode for days afterwards, to George's irritation, but he eventually came to see the humor in it."

"You've had some good times up here, haven't you?" she said, laughing at the story.

"Yes, I have," he said thoughtfully, "and there's going to be many more to come."

They were still chuckling about his story when they topped a rise and found themselves looking down at the Florida River—one of the smaller rivers of the area. It ran almost parallel to the Pine River on the east and the Animas on the west. It originated high in the mountains northeast of Animas City and Durango, Colorado. In fact, later it would become the principal water source for both communities. Supplies and materials would be packed in by mules and burros to a place high in the mountains just below its headwaters. A small settlement was built to house the workers and a reservoir was constructed to provide sufficient water for the growing towns it served.

Morgan had followed the Florida from its very beginnings at a little pond down over the face of a granite dome, passed the place that was to become the man-made lake, on down its lovely valley until it eventually emptied into the Animas River a few miles north of New Mexico. He had found some gold in it, but the real treasure it offered was the majestic scenery and pools teeming with mountain trout. There were places on it's way south where the river cut through small, narrow slits in the solid rock not much wider than the river bed itself. It was impossible for a horse to navigate these places, so he would have to go on foot. Crossing continually back and forth, climbing up around water falls and long stretches of cascading torrents, one could fish or pan to his heart's content. At times he would stop and just stare straight up the sheer rock faces that lined the river bank. He had often wondered how deep these canyons were. Several hundred feet, he figured.

One time he was in the canyon just north of what was to become Transfer Park. This little meadow had gotten its name because when they were building the lake up the river this was the spot where they transferred the materials from the wagons to the back of mules and burros, as wagons could go no farther. Anyway, he was in the middle of the canyon and a storm came up. It was a good old mountain cloudburst. Water was coming down in sheets between the sheer walls of rock engulfing the river. Then something happened that was breath-taking as well as terrifying. Lightning would strike down in the canyon and bounce back and forth between the rock walls. It was in the middle of the afternoon but the storm made it almost dark. When the lightning would strike, it would illuminate the canyon brighter than day and the deafening claps of thunder added to the magnificence of the occasion. Yes, this small river had provided him with many memories. Those memories flooded back as he and Rose worked their way down the steep hillside to the river below. She seemed to enjoy his stories, so he talked all the way down. By the time they reached the river, Morgan figured it was about four in the afternoon, by the look of the sun. Plenty of time to set up the camp and catch a nice mess of trout for their last supper on the trail.

He found the place that he had camped several times in the past. It offered excellent shelter in case of rain and had an eastern exposure, so the sun would hit it fairly early in the morning. The river was a stone's throw away and the running water would provide a pleasant melody for them on their last night out. After setting up camp and taking care of the horses. he headed for the stream. It wasn't long until he had enough trout for the main course. He was almost back to camp when he heard the scream. There was a sense of urgency in that scream.

Running as fast as he could, he tore through the camp, dropping the fish near the fire. Calling out, he needed to find out where she was. About that time, he heard a ruckus back in a grove of wild berry bushes. Arriving on the scene, he found Rose standing with her back up against a tree holding a pan of freshly picked berries. Standing in front of her, about twenty feet away, was the biggest black bear that Morgan had seen in a long while.

"Stand still, Rose," he said quietly as he reached her and gently took hold of her arm. "Be very still."

His right hand went down and pulled out his six-gun. He didn't want to fire unless he had to. He didn't figure he could kill it with a six-shooter, but maybe he could scare the critter off with it. The bear dropped down on all fours and came a few feet closer. Then, standing up on his hind legs, he let out a roar as if he meant business. He had no sooner let out a second roar when the dog lit right in the middle of his back. The bear let out a roar, shaking the dog off and sending him rolling, and then turned to meet his attacker.

"Don't let Dawg get hurt!" Rose pleaded with Morgan.

"Don't worry about Dawg, Rose, he knows how to take care of himself. Better worry about us. I don't think we can outrun that bear."

Meanwhile the dog was running round and round the bear, darting in and out, grabbing a chunk of hair now and then. The last time he darted in, the bear was ready. Catching him in mid-air with one of his paws, he sent the dog sprawling. *Time to put a stop to this,* Morgan thought, and pointing his six-gun in the air, he fired off a couple of shots. The startled bear took off down the trail. Just to make sure he kept going, the man fired a couple more rounds. Running over to the limp dog, Rose knelt down by him.

"Is he all right?" she asked, as the man felt the dog's rib cage.

"I think so. Probably only has the breath knocked out of him, and there's a little piece of hide torn loose, but it's not that bad." The dog started coming to and gradually got up. "Yes, he'll be okay, it'll take more than an old bear to do him in. Let's get him back to camp and put some salve on that tear, though he'll probably lick it off."

"Thank you ,boy," she said as she gave him a big hug.

"Not too hard,' Morgan cautioned, almost envious of the dog, "his ribs are more than likely sore."

Getting back to camp, Morgan got the fish ready while Rose took care of the dog. The sun had just set and twilight was coming on as they sat down to eat. During the meal, Rose talked about the berries and how the bear had scared her silly. The dog, not feeling too good, had laid down at her feet and was taking a nap. Out of the clear blue, Rose spoke up.

"Really, Fletcher, why haven't you ever married?"

Almost choking on a bite of fish, he looked up with a startled look on his face. "What in the world brought that on?"

"I don't really know,' she said, blushing. "It just popped into my head, I guess."

"Well, it's easy to answer. That's just the way it is." He grinned at her, which added to the reddening of her face.

Regaining her composure, she came back. "Is it because you've never found a mountain woman who would live up here in the hills with you?"

"No, that's not the way it is. The plain simple truth is that I've never run into anyone I wanted to get hitched up with, and I'm not going to get married just for the sake of being married, that's for sure. So I haven't even come close to tying the knot."

"You mean to tell me you've never gotten close to any woman?" She gave him an *I can't believe it* look.

"Nope, I'm not saying that at all. There is a woman that I like a lot and I'm close to personally."

"Do you mind if I ask who, or is it none of my business?"

"I don't mind a bit," he said as he reached over and threw a log on the fire. Turning back to Rose, he continued. "In fact, Sally Wiggins is her name. Remember I mentioned her once when we were talking. She runs a boarding house down in Durango."

Thinking for a minute, she remembered. "She nursed you back to health one winter a few years ago. Right?"

"Yes, that's the one."

"What makes you feel so close to her?" Her curiosity got the best of her.

"Several things, I guess," Morgan said thoughtfully. "She's a good friend and she has been ever since I was a kid. She's one of the few people who really understands me. Why I do the things I do and why I'm like I am. She's always told me to find out what I really want out of life and go get it. Not to let public opinion influence me to be something I didn't want to be."

Rose interrupted him. "Do you feel I have been trying to influence you to do something you don't want to do?"

"Of course not," he said, shaking his head. "You've expressed some strong feelings as to what's important in your life and how you feel about certain things. Maybe you influenced me some, but I can't say that's all bad. In fact, you've given me some things to ponder, but I'm not going to do anything I don't want to do, you can depend on that!"

"Please believe me when I say that I'm not trying to pressure you in any way. I would never want to do that." She hoped he knew that.

"I know," he assured her, "and I guess that's why I think so much of Sally. She never pressured me on anything either. She was just there when I was hurting or needed someone's shoulder to cry on."

"Maybe you should have married her," Rose said, feeling a pang of jealousy.

"No, that wouldn't have worked at all," Morgan replied, without bothering to explain that Sally was thirty years older than he and had been more like a mother to him since his own mother died.

Rose fell silent for awhile, thinking things over. It bothered her that she had felt envious of Sally. She looked at Morgan across the fire as it was dying and the flickering flames caused weird looking shadows to jump across his face. She was certainly grateful for what he had done for her and she admired the kind of man he was, but were those feelings turning into something more than gratitude? She was strangely drawn to him in a way she had never experienced before. She was feeling emotions she had never had before.

"Any more questions on why I'm not married?" he asked her, a mischievous smile covering his face. Only half-way listening to him, she shook her head.

"Well, then, tell me why *you* aren't married."

That question brought her back to reality. She sat there with her mouth wide open. It was a subject she was sensitive about and generally wouldn't discuss it. But fair was fair. She had opened the door and now felt obliged to answer.

"Well, I guess there are several reasons why. For one, like you, I haven't met anyone I've wanted to marry.....for another, I wouldn't make a good wife."

"Wait a minute," Morgan objected. "I don't believe that for a minute—that last part, I mean,"

"It's true. Around here, good men need strong, healthy women for wives. It takes two hard-working people to make a life, to have a family and build something worth having. I've always been sort of frail and weak and I could never pull my weight in such a marriage. Furthermore, I'm not going to be a pretty showpiece for some wealthy dude in some city. I have a hard time respecting that kind of man. Fletcher, when I marry, it will be for love. To a man who can accept me for what I am and not for what I can contribute, though I will give it all I've got."

"The right man could never ask for more than that, Rose."

"I've wondered if there ever will be the right man, though when I was a bit younger there was a boy who was fond of me. I know he accepted me for what I was, and I sort of liked him too. He grew up to be a great person and he works as a storekeeper in a trading post near the ranch."

"What happened between you?" Morgan wondered.

"Brad," was her reply. "Brad, my brother, just wouldn't let it happen. He couldn't accept the fact that this guy was a storekeeper and, as such, was not good enough for his sister. He made it so tough on Jerry that he just gave up. I guess it was just as well. I doubt if I could have ever loved him."

Morgan sensed that she didn't want to talk about it further so he interrupted her thoughts. "Well, it's time to hit the old sack. We need to get an earlier start than we did this morning."

"You're right," she said, "I'm tired." With that, she got her bedroll ready and settled down for the night. It would give her a chance to do some thinking before going to sleep.

Morgan went out and checked the horses. The moon was up and still almost full. The sky was clear and the stars were shining in all their glory. The air was almost completely still and it would get nippy tonight. He thought it best to gather up some extra wood to keep the fire going. He wanted Rose to be comfortable on her last night with him in the wilds.

He couldn't get rid of the feeling that they were being watched. Though he had seen no sign of anyone, he could feel the presence of someone out there in the dark. And what about that gunfire, he asked himself again. Well, no use worrying about it. If something happened, he'd just have to handle it the best he knew how.

Fourteen

Morgan was up just before daylight. He wanted to get breakfast out of the way so they could get an early start. Soon a cooking fire was blazing, the coffee cooling, and the last of their camp meat was sizzling in the frying pan. While it cooked, Morgan was busy mixing up the biscuit dough and as soon as the biscuits were done, it was gravy time. Just the thought of it put his mouth to watering. Bending down over Rose's bedroll, he gently shook her.

"Rise and shine, sleepyhead," he said softly. "It's time to hit the trail."

Slowly raising up she let out a big yawn and stretched. "Do we have to hurry?" she asked.

"Yes, this is the big day," he answered. "We'll be in Durango late this afternoon and we can wire your folks of your return, clean up and enjoy a home cooked meal at the Boarding House this evening."

"Where's Dawg?" she asked.

"I don't know," he replied. "He was gone when I got up, but he'll be back once he gets a whiff of breakfast cooking."

They had just finished eating when the dog showed up. He was nervous and the hair was slightly raised on his back. Keeping back some biscuits and a piece of meat for each of them, Morgan gave the dog what was left of the food and told him to settle down. Finally they were ready. Morgan had decided it would be best to follow the river downstream until they came to Horse Gulch and there they would meet up with the Pagosa Springs road, which would take them on into Durango. Though there had been a light frost during the night, all indications pointed to a clear, warm day. The air was still, with only an occasional gust of breeze that left a refreshing fall feeling. As the rays from the rising sun hit the Florida, the reflections bouncing off the running water gave the appearance of a million diamonds sparkling on the water as it playfully made its way downstream.

What a beautiful day, Morgan was thinking to himself, but he couldn't shake the feeling of doom he had. He was sure they had been followed ever since leaving the cave. There was not only his feeling, but the actions of the dog only confirmed his own misgivings. At noon they stopped at the side of the river close to a little meadow where the horses could rest and eat their fill of grass. Making a pot of coffee, they ate the leftover biscuits from breakfast and finished off the last of the dried venison.

Rose stretched out on her blanket and took a short nap. Morgan wasn't napping. He was staring at the running water, deep in thought. He was sure this time that he had made up his mind. It was clear to him, at least at the moment, what he was going to do with the rest of his life, but was it *really* settled in his mind? But first things first. He needed to get Rose home, making sure nothing happened in the few short miles left. After they reached Durango, he knew for sure what he was going to do. He would discuss his plan with her on the way into Durango this afternoon.

It wasn't long after they broke camp that they came to Horse Gulch. The trail that they were following came close to the river at this point. It was here that it met up with the road that ran between Pagosa and Durango. They would turn right on it and it would only be six or seven miles before they could enjoy a hot bath and a home-cooked meal at the boarding house in Durango.

"Let's stop for a few minutes and water the horses and stretch the old legs," Morgan said as he slid off the rump of Blue. After helping Rose dismount, he took the canteen off Millie's pack and handed it to her. She had just started to take a drink when Dawg bristled up and went to growling. Morgan followed his gaze across the river.

A big black horse was emerging from among the aspens. The rider, proudly holding his head high, advanced to the edge of the river bank. Except for a knife, he was unarmed. As the black pranced, Two Bears held up his arm in a gesture of peace.

"I was wondering when he was going to show up," Morgan said softly, without taking his gaze from the Indian. "Here," he said, taking his rifle out of the scabbard and handing it to Rose. "Stay close to Millie. I'm going to see what he has to say." He looked down at the dog. "Stay with Rose," he commanded as he mounted Blue and started for the river bank. As Blue stopped on the west side of the river, the two men sized each other up for a minute or two. The Indian broke the silence.

"I am called Two Bears."

"My name is Fletcher Morgan."

"Let there be peace between us, Fletcher Morgan," Two Bears said, holding his arm up once more as if to emphasize his intentions.

Returning the gesture, Morgan replied, "There is peace." After several moments of silence, Morgan continued, "You speak good English, Two Bears."

"It is well to know the tongue of your enemy," replied Two Bears.

"Am I your enemy?"

"All white men are my enemies. You, I honor and make peace because of my grandfather's word."

"Your grandfather?"

"Yes, it was he who gave you the blue horse that you ride. He told us all that you were a good white man and no harm should come to you from our people. I did not know this when I fired on you. At that time, I saw the horse and, because I was careless, you wounded me. It is no matter. The wound will heal."

"Well," Morgan said with a grin, "on the night this all got started, you shot me in the arm. I guess that makes us even....I remember your grandfather. Is he well?"

"He is getting old and it is hard for him to see, but he is well. It is his wish that you come sit and talk with him. He is going to spend the winter at the agency in Ignacio."

"That I can and will do," promised Morgan. "What is your grandfather's name?"

"Ask for 'He who speaks wisdom' and everyone knows where he will be." There was silence for what seemed an eternity to Morgan. There was only the sound of the running water in the river and a snort from Millie as she impatiently stomped the ground. Suddenly Two Bears spoke. "Is she your woman?"

Morgan measured his words carefully as he looked around at Rose. Turning back to Two Bears he answered firmly, "Yes, she is my woman."

"Then it is done," Two Bears replied. "I will bother you no more." Two Bears nudged the black and started to turn away.

"Wait, Two Bears," Morgan said, "there's something I need to know." Stopping the black and turning to face Morgan, Two Bears waited patiently. "The gunfire two evenings ago—what was it about?"

"Your enemies had started to follow you. There is no need to worry. They will bother you no more."

Morgan didn't need to be told what that meant. "I will not tell anyone, but if the Army finds out, they will hunt you down. You know you can't win, Two Bears. You can't keep fighting the white man and live."

"I would rather die than live many years being pushed around by those who have taken our home from my people. May you live in peace, Fletcher Morgan, but I must continue my fight." With those words, Two Bears turned and slowly disappeared into the forest.

Turning Blue, Morgan returned to where Rose and the others waited. Putting the rifle away and helping Rose up into the saddle, he swung up behind her. "Did you hear what he said?" he asked her.

"Yes, I did," she replied "and it makes me sad."

"Well, I wish him the best. It's for sure he thinks he's in the right and, who knows, maybe he is." He paused. "Only six or seven more miles to go," he said as they started up the little canyon.

"What happens when we get to town?" she asked.

"I've been thinking about that," Morgan replied. "I was going to go with you on the stage to Aztec and make sure you got home safely, but I think we'll change that plan, that is, if you agree. I have some urgent business I need to tend to."

"Okay," she said, "so what's the plan now?"

"First of all, I'm going to get someone to go from Durango to Aztec with you. If you are agreeable, I will ask Sally to go with you. That way you will have some company. To make sure you don't get lost again, I'm going to ask the marshal to send a man with you ladies. He'll do it, since he owes me a favor or two."

Oh, great, he's sending Sally, she thought, and then said aloud, "Is this business real important?"

"I think it is," he said quite seriously.

"I wish very much that you would take me home so you could meet my family and they could thank you personally. But if this business is that important to you, go ahead and I'll go with Sally."

"It *is* very important," he emphasized, "and thank you for understanding."

"But you have to promise me that as soon as your business is done, you'll come and meet my family."

"You bet your life I will and you've got my word on it," he said. The truth was that wild horses couldn't keep him away!

The sun was starting to slip behind Smelter Mountain when the travelers came out of Horse Gulch and caught sight of the buildings of Durango. Durango was a newly built railroad town and it lay in the river valley surrounded on the east and west by mountains. The town had been built right on the banks of the *El Rio de Las Animas Perdidas,* Spanish for 'River of Lost Souls', more commonly known as the Animas. Its headwaters were high in the San Juan Mountains northeast of Baker's Park, later known as Silverton. It gains momentum as it runs south through the narrow, rugged Animas Canyon and then slows down as it enters a long spacious valley farther downstream. Several tributaries fed it and contributed to its size as one of the largest waterways in the area. Near Baker's Park, Mineral Creek joins it and further south, in the rugged canyon, Cascade adds its water. In the serene valley below the canyon, Hermosa, Lightner, and Junction Creeks contribute still more to its size. Eventually it meets up with the San Juan River about thirty miles into New Mexico.

Several notable towns had sprung up on its banks. To the north, there was Silverton, which was an enduring settlement. It resulted from the silver rush that caused mines to spring up everywhere in the mountains surrounding it. Going south, after the river leaves its narrow, rocky canyon and suddenly emerges into the long valley, several small communities burst forth, but none survived or amounted to much.

A few miles farther south, just where the river makes a bend, Animas City was born. It was conceived as a farming and ranching center. Through sheer determination, its founders made it a thriving trade center, knowing well that the miners and Indians would need the produce and supplies they could furnish. Around 1880 the railroad was planning to build a line up this scenic valley to Silverton to tap the rich resources of that area. The City Fathers of Animas City refused to let them make their town into a railroad stop, especially since the railroad wanted to do it on their terms, so Animas City stubbornly stuck to their guns to preserve it as an agricultural community. The determined railroad built its own town. Moving just two miles south of Animas City, they laid out a town site and called it Durango. Durango grew rapidly and eventually it swallowed up its northern neighbor, Animas City, and in time became the principal Colorado settlement on the river.

About twenty miles south of the Colorado line, another settlement was being formed. It became known as Aztec, named after the Indian ruins that it bordered. Here the Animas curved westward to meet the San Juan. At that junction, another town sprang up that came to be known as Farmington. These two valleys, the Animas and the San Juan, though bordered on the south by desert country, became productive farming and ranching communities, noted for their orchards and fruit-producing qualities.

As Morgan and Rose came out of Horse Gulch, they followed the road to the railway station. Then turning north, they headed up Main Street in Durango.

"At last, we made it," he said excitedly to Rose.

"Where's Dawg?" Rose asked, looking all around. "Where'd he go?"

"He stopped when we came out of Horse Gulch. You were so busy looking around that you didn't notice. He won't come into town, but he'll hang around the edge of it until I leave and then he'll pick me up. Like I said before, he hates people in general."

"Well, I will want to see him before I leave," Rose said emphatically.

"Don't worry," Morgan promised. "I'll see that you do."

"Hey, there's Taylor's new store. After we're settled, I'll take you down to meet him." Turning the corner that the bank was on, they pulled the horses up in front of a two story boarding house. Dismounting, he helped Rose off and tied the horses to the hitching rail. "Well, we're back in civilization at last," he declared as he swept his arm in a long gesture covering the town. "Did you ever think we'd make it?"

"Never doubted it for a moment," she replied with a smug look on her face. "Not with you leading the way!"

"Let's go see what old Sal is doing," Morgan said with a wink.

Opening the front door very quietly, the two stepped into a large parlor. Down the hallway and from the first door on the right, they could hear the humming of a woman. Taking hold of Rose's hand and moving very quietly, Morgan headed in the direction of the open door leading into the kitchen. Standing at the sink with her back to the door was a large, well-built woman doing the supper dishes. As they stood just inside the door, Morgan said in a low voice, "Supper ready yet?"

For a moment the woman stood there motionless and then suddenly whirled around. "Fletcher Morgan!" she cried. "I'd know that voice anywhere!" She ran up and gave him a big bear hug and kissed him on the cheek. "Where have you been? I haven't seen you in months. Let me look at you," she said, holding him at arms length. Then she gave him another hug.

"Oh, I've been up in the mountains roaming around, as usual, but this time I found something, Sal," he said, turning her to face Rose.

For the first time, Rose got a good look at the woman she had had jealousy pains over. She was a good-looking woman, probably in her middle fifties with shoulder length hair that had started to gray.

"And who is this?" Sally asked as she studied the young lady standing before her dressed in men's pants and shirt, wearing moccasins.

"Sal, meet Roseanna Jackson, my newly found friend. Rose, meet my old friend, Sally Wiggins."

"Glad to meet you, honey," Sally said, giving her a hug too.

"It sure is good to meet you, Miss Wiggins. Fletcher has told me many things about you," Rose replied, hugging the older woman back. "But not everything," she said under her breath.

Stepping back and holding Rose by her shoulders at arms length, Sally jokingly said, "I hope some of it was good and, by the way, my friends call me Sal."

"Thank you, Sal," Rose replied, turning to Morgan. "I like your friend a lot, even the part you left out."

"Hold the fort!" Sally suddenly exclaimed. "Did I hear you right? Did you say Roseanna Jackson? Not the same Roseanna Jackson that was kidnapped and everyone is looking for!"

"The very same," Morgan answered. "We met up at a Ute pow-wow and I decided to take her with me. We've been trying to get her home ever since."

"But how? When, where?" Sally quickly asked.

"Hold on," Morgan said, putting his arm around her shoulders. "Feed us some supper and we'll fill you in on the whole story."

"Well, sit down! I have plenty of grub left over. You two must be starved!"

"Wait a minute," Morgan said as he turned toward the door. "I'd better go take care of the horses. They're hungry and thirsty, too. Go ahead and eat, Rose, and I'll grab a bite when I get back."

"That's fine with us," Sally ventured. "It'll give us ladies a chance to talk and get to know each other, but don't take too long."

"I won't," Morgan assured her. "Rose, if the telegraph station is still open, I think I'll send your father a wire telling him that you're okay and when he needs to pick you up from the stage stop."

"I would appreciate that. I'd like them to know as soon as possible," Rose said and then added, "When will I get to Aztec?"

"That's a good question. Sal, when does the next stage leave for Aztec?" he asked his friend.

"Let's see....day after tomorrow, if I remember correctly....Yes, early Wednesday morning."

"Got it!" he said as he left to take care of the horses.

The livery stable was a couple of blocks down the side street from the boarding house, just on the edge of town. He made arrangements for the animals and he stored his gear. He took his saddlebags, making sure his extra gun and what little gold he had found during the summer was inside them. Grabbing his rifle, he started down the street to the telegraph office to send the wire. Going inside, he gave the following message to the old gentleman at the keyboard:

> *To J.J. Jackson...J bar J Ranch...Aztec, New Mexico*
> *Roseanna found and is safe...Will arrive on the*
> *Wednesday stage from Durango...Please meet*
> *her...Fletcher Morgan.*

After making sure the message had been sent and received, he returned to the boarding house. He found the women busy talking and having a big time. Sal filled his plate and poured him a cup of coffee.

"What's this I hear?" she started before he could get the first bite in his mouth. "You're not going to take Roseanna on to Aztec and deliver her to her parents personally?"

"Yep, that's what I was thinking," he replied, grinning back at her. "I have something really important to take care of and I'm running out of time. By the way, what's the date? How many more days until the first of October?"

"Three," Sally answered, "but is it so important that you can't take a few days and see this girl home?"

"I'm afraid it is. You know I wouldn't do it this way if it wasn't," he said seriously. "But that's where you come in, Sal. I was hoping you would go with Rose and see that she gets safely home." Seeing the look on her face, he pleaded, "It's important! I need to make a decision and I want to talk to an old man first."

"Okay....*okay*!" she conceded. "I'll do it, but you owe me one."

"I owe you far more than that. Thank you very much." Between mouthfuls, he added, "I hope you have room to put us up for a couple of nights."

"Well, we are full, but Roseanna can stay with me in my room and you can use the spare room I keep especially for times like this." Then turning back to Rose, "Now, dear, tell me the rest of the story and then you can take a long, hot bath and get into some clothes fit for a lady instead of that mountain garb you have on."

The next morning after breakfast, Morgan went down to the marshal's office. He explained to Jim Clark the situation with Rose and asked if he had a man he could send with the two women the next day. Clark assured him it would be no problem and he would have someone at the stage by the time it left Wednesday morning. Walking back down to the livery stable, he checked on the horses. While he was there he rented a horse and buggy and by the time he got back to the boarding house, it was midmorning.

Rose and Sally were sitting at the table talking and sipping coffee. He couldn't help staring at Rose all dressed up in a light brown dress. She was beautiful. The dress set off her auburn hair and emerald eyes. There was no doubt that she was a bonafide lady! He sat down and poured himself a fresh cup.

"Well, ladies, if you are about finished gossiping, I'd like to take this beautiful lady and give her a grand tour of my hometown.

I got a buggy so we can go in style."

"I'd love that!" Rose said, sliding back her chair and getting up. "Can we go now?"

"The sooner the better, " he replied. "Just let me finish my coffee."

"When shall I plan on you two being back?" Sally asked.

"Oh, about suppertime, I guess," he replied. "I want to go by the old place and then see Taylor. We'll probably visit with him awhile."

"I'll have supper ready for you whenever you get back. So get out of here!"

Morgan helped Rose into the buggy and then turned it around, heading north towards Animas City. It was a warm autumn day and there were scattered clouds that blocked out the sun briefly at times. There was a slight breeze blowing and it had a crisp, fresh feel. Yes, it was a delightful day for sightseeing. A short distance separated the two communities and soon they were crossing the bridge over the river into Animas City. The old blacksmith shop looked the same as when it was a part of his life. Morgan asked the smithy if it would be all right for them to see the house. Showing Rose the shop and the house brought a lot of pleasant memories back to his mind, but the bad ones came flooding in on him too. They must have walked the neighborhood for a couple of hours as he recounted some of his memories of home and the way it used to be.

Getting back into the buggy, he headed towards the store Taylor owned in Animas City. Arriving there he was told that Taylor was at the other store in Durango. Heading back towards Durango, Morgan took her down along the Animas river, visiting some of the places where he had spent time fishing with his father and then having a picnic with the whole family at end of day. It felt good for him to share these memories with someone like Rose. It seemed to take away many of the bitter feelings. As Morgan and Rose entered the mercantile store, Taylor was waiting.

"Hello, big brother," he said with a smile on his face, pumping Fletcher's hand up and down. "I heard this morning that you were back in town." Turning to Rose, he grasped her hand. "And this must be the famous lady you rescued!"

"Boy, news sure gets around here fast!" Morgan said as he gave Taylor a big hug, lifting him off the floor and turning around and around.

"Put me down and let's go back to the office and visit awhile."

They spent the rest of the afternoon bringing each other up to date on all the latest. Finally, about six o'clock, they said good-bye to Taylor and went back to the boarding house.

"The stage leaves at nine in the morning so if you want to see the dog again, we'll have to leave a little early for the station," Morgan said, as he opened the front door of the boarding house for her.

"Yes, I want to see Dawg. Are you sure you know where he is?"

"Don't worry, I know."

Fifteen

The next morning Sally had breakfast ready at daylight. The woman who was going to take care of the boarding house while Sally was gone helped her and Rose get ready for their trip south. Morgan went and got the buggy and by seven-thirty they were on their way. Morgan took Main Street south and headed towards Horse Gulch. As they started up into the gulch, he stopped the horses and let out a loud whistle. It wasn't but a few minutes until the dog made his appearance.

Rose knelt down and Dawg came up to her. She gave him a hug and stroked his head and back, talking to him as if he were her kid.

"I've seen everything now," Sally said in disbelief. "She's the first person I've seen that dog get close to."

"Yep," Morgan replied, "they hit it off from the very start and it's the dangest thing I've ever seen, too."

Finally Morgan walked up to where Rose and the dog were. "It's time to go or you'll miss the stage."

"You'll bring him when you come see me, won't you?" she asked as she gave him a final hug.

"He'll be with me, you can bet on that. I don't think I'm going to lose him anytime soon." Then he looked down at Dawg. "See you later," he said as he turned the buggy around and headed back to the stage stop.

The man from the marshal's office was waiting when they arrived. Morgan didn't know him, but Sally did, and she assured Morgan that he was all right. The stage had pulled up and was loading the few things for delivery in Aztec. Sally and the deputy boarded but Rose stayed behind with Morgan for a few minutes.

"You won't forget to come and see me, will you?" she asked as she turned toward him and looked up into his eyes.

"It may be a couple of weeks but I'll come, that's for sure," he promised.

Without saying another word, she raised up on her tiptoes and tenderly kissed him on the lips. Then turning, without a sound or a look-back, she walked to the stage and got in.

"Haw, haw, you nags," the driver yelled as he gave the reins a brisk snap. The stage turned and headed south along Main Street and Rose was on her way to the long-awaited reunion with her family. Morgan stared at it until it disappeared down the Animas River Valley.

Returning the buggy to the livery, he saddled Blue and got ready to leave. He would leave Millie here until he returned, taking only the bare necessities for the short trip. Soon he had Blue packed and ready to go. He had one last stop to make on his way out of town. Hitching Blue in front of the bank, he went in and spent some time talking with the banker. Coming out, he mounted and started for Horse Gulch to pick up Dawg.

****

It was ten days later when Morgan approached Aztec, New Mexico. At the north end of town he stopped by the river and left the dog off.

"I'll be back tomorrow," he told Dawg as Blue started towards town.

Riding down the center of town he pulled up at what served as a barber shop and went in. There was no one in the shop except a small skinny man with a handlebar mustache.

"What'll it be, stranger?" he asked in a cheerful way.

"Need a hair cut and a shave," Morgan replied as he sat down in the chair.

"Just passing through?" the barber asked as he started to work on Morgan.

"Guess you could say that," was the muffled reply. "By the way, how's a fellow get to the J bar J Ranch?"

"That's easy. Just ride southeast. Just before you reach the San Juan, turn to your left and follow the road. Can't miss it." After a pause, he continued curiously, "You a friend of Mr. Jackson?"

"Never met the man."

"You'll like J.J. He's one fine man," the barber offered and although he wanted to pry, he thought better of it.

"I've heard that, and from a pretty reliable source. I'm looking forward to meeting him."

"You don't have to ride clear out there to meet him. You can go to the pie supper the town's having down at the Community

Hall this evening. The community is celebrating the return of the Jackson girl, you know, the one that was kidnapped. It turns out that some mountain man found her and brought her in. Her brothers just got back from the mountains. They were out there hunting her and now everyone is going to have a big get-together and celebrate."

"Where's this Community Hall located?" Morgan asked.

"Down at the end of the street on the right."

"You wouldn't have a place I could take a bath?" Morgan asked as he got out of the barber chair.

"Sure do. The tub's in the back room. Go on in and I'll get some hot water."

After finishing up with the barber, Morgan walked Blue across the street to a little hotel. After signing the register, he asked the clerk about a place to bed Blue down. The clerk informed him there was a stable of sorts behind the hotel. Taking the horse, he fixed him up for the night. Then it was back to his room where he laid down for a short nap. It must have been seven o'clock when he woke up. Putting on the brand new clothes he had bought in Durango, he strapped on his six-gun and was ready to go. It would be interesting to see how things would turn out when he made known his plans.

As he approached the Hall, he could hear the music. It sounded good to him. It had been a while since he had gone to a shindig. Stepping quietly into the bright light, he quickly surveyed the surroundings. The band was at the far end of a big open room. There were a couple of guitars, a piano, and a fiddle. Several couples were dancing. On the left, against the wall, was a row of chairs, most of them full, and on this end of the room they had set up a table stacked high with pies. At the far end of the pie table, with her back to him, stood Rose. The band had finished a two-step and had started a waltz as Morgan walked toward her. Stopping just behind her, he spoke.

"I believe this is my dance."

Whirling around, a big smile came to her face and with tear-filled eyes, she replied, "Yes, it is, kind sir." With that, she held out her arms to him.

"You'll have to excuse my dancing," he said. "I'm not too refined when it comes to this." Then he took her in his arms and started to waltz.

"I don't mind a bit," she replied. "You will do just fine." They waltzed for a bit as if they were the only ones on the floor. Finally he spoke.

"I've missed you."

"I know," she answered softly. "I've missed you too."

"I bought the ranch," he said.

"I know," she replied.

"I bought it for us to share."

"I know."

"Does that mean you'll marry me?"

"Yes."

They danced for a moment in silence and she laid her head on his shoulder. Then, teasingly, she added, "You'll have to tell my father and my brothers!"

"I know," he replied with a sigh.

"You may get some resistance."

"I know...but I think I can handle it."

"I have no doubt." She looked up into his eyes and a little smile crossed her lips as she spoke. "Just think, this all happened because you rescued me."

"Yep," he replied, "but I'm a bit confused as to who rescued who." He was silent for a moment and then he continued as they waltzed around the dance floor. "It's been a long, hard ride...but I'm home now."

The Rescue of Fletcher Morgan Order Form

Use this convenient order form to order additional copies of
The Rescue of Fletcher Morgan

Please Print:

Name_____

Address_____

City_____ **State**_____

Zip_____

Phone(   )_____

    ___ copies of book @ $9.95 each $_____
Postage and handling @ $2.95 per book $_____
NM residents add 6.25% tax $_____
Total amount enclosed $_____

Make checks payable to Gary D. Oliver

Send to Gary D. Oliver
#4 CR 2891
Aztec, NM 87410

Self-Love 365 Days

365 Days of Daily Self-Love Affirmations

Written by Elena Elin

© **Copyright 2017 - All rights reserved.**

The contents of this book may not be reproduced, duplicated or transmitted without direct written permission from the author.

Under no circumstances will any legal responsibility or blame be held against the publisher for any reparation, damages, or monetary loss due to the information herein, either directly or indirectly.

Legal Notice:

This book is copyright protected. This is only for personal use. You cannot amend, distribute, sell, use, quote or paraphrase any part or the content within this book without the consent of the author.

Disclaimer Notice:

Please note the information contained within this document is for educational and entertainment purposes only. Every attempt has been made to provide accurate, up to date and reliable complete information. No warranties of any kind are expressed or implied. Readers acknowledge that the author is not engaging in the rendering of legal, financial, medical or professional advice. The content of this book has been derived from various sources. Please consult a licensed professional before attempting any techniques outlined in this book.

By reading this document, the reader agrees that under no circumstances are is the author responsible for any losses, direct or indirect, which are incurred as a result of the use of information contained within this document, including, but not limited to, —errors, omissions, or inaccuracies.

Table of Contents

Introduction 1

Chapter 1 – January 3

Chapter 2 – February 11

Chapter 3 – March... 17

Chapter 4 – April 23

Chapter 5 – May 29

Chapter 6 – June 35

Chapter 7 – July 41

Chapter 8 – August... 47

Chapter 9 – September 53

Chapter 10 – October 59

Chapter 11 - November 65

Chapter 12 – December 71

Conclusion 77

Introduction

Isn't it enough that people around you love you? You may have asked yourself this, but all love that is worth having starts with self-love. If you don't love yourself, what chances do you have of having others really love you? When you are able to love yourself, you are at a stage when people will love you as well because you are making the most of whom you are. You are enjoying your life and valuing your body and mind and unless your value them, how can you ever expect any form of happiness to be consistent?

In this book of 365 affirmations – we have taken events through the calendar year and have made special affirmations that you can use to get you through your year in a positive state of mind. We have also explained their significance because it isn't just about saying positive things to yourself. It's about believing them with all your heart so that you come over to others as a loving and complete person whose belief in self is without question.

Introduction

Once you are able to achieve that, the world is your oyster. You will be able to win friends. You will be able to steer a course in your life and become whoever it is that you want to become. We are only limited when we step away from self-love and try to please others rather than ourselves. You can actually do both, but the self-love part comes first. Being comfortable in the skin you're in will allow you to offer so much more to every relationship you ever have. You will impress people because they will want to emulate you and be like you.

You only need to look at your own heroes and heroines to know that they are stars in your mind because of who they are. Become who you want to be because it's really as simple as understanding what self-love is all about and then exercising it in your everyday life. Step through the pages on a daily basis and enjoy the next year of positivity and self-love. When you make affirmations, you increase the potential of your own success. These stay in your mind and help you to aim high in your life so that you never make the mistake of forgetting your purpose, which is to embrace self-love. Follow the months, through the seasons and start to increase your awareness of what life has on offer.

Chapter 1 – January

At the end of each chapter, you will find the affirmations that have been written especially for you for each month of the year. January is a time when it may be particularly cold. Perhaps the world doesn't look as kindly as it could upon health questions. Perhaps you don't have the money for sufficient heating. Perhaps you are fed up of having to dress up in many layers just to keep warm. However, that shouldn't affect the way you feel about yourself and your life.

At the very beginning of January, you woke up having made resolutions for the New Year and then woke up to a new year and a new start. What better time to start on the self-love trail? New Year's Eve brought out that reflection on your life; on the changes that you need to make, in order to make your life happier and healthier in the coming year. Thus, the affirmations in this chapter begin with those that cover the resolutions that you made and help to reinforce them. As we go through the month, they also

Chapter 1 – January

relate to changes that the New Year means to you. For example, if you have been putting off doing things that you know will benefit you, now is the time to begin again and to go into these aspects of your life with belief in yourself. You get that belief by knowing that what you are thinking about yourself is positive and that you will put your best effort into looking after your body and mind over the next year in order to maximize your own potential as a human being. If you have never really believed in yourself, now is the time to start.

I would suggest that in conjunction with the affirmations made for January, you also learn to meditate. There's a very powerful reason for this. Meditation helps you to be able to feel at ease and have a great mind body connection that encourages self-love. It isn't anything that will encourage ego. Loving yourself and being selfish are two very different things. When you are selfish you put your needs before the needs of people around you and people who love themselves don't do that. They love who they are because they are able to better serve their communities, because they are better able to balance their lives and are altogether happier in themselves.

So how do you meditate and how often should you do it. You should meditate daily because if you don't, you won't get that good at it. Sit down on a hard chair and place your feet flat on the floor. Learn to breathe in through the nostrils and hold the breath for a moment, before breathing out. When you meditate, all that you do is concentrate on the breath. You don't think about anything else. You breathe in, hold, breathe out and then count one. You breathe in, hold, breathe out and then count two, etc. until you reach ten, but there is a snag. If you start to find other thoughts entering your head, you have to go back to one again.

You will find that the better you get at meditation, the better able you will be to love yourself and to use that self-love in a very distinct way for the betterment of your life, your dreams and hopes and for the assistance of others. It isn't just about you. In this world, you have to interact with people and meditation helps you to calmly accept all those things you are unable to change. You accept diversity instead of fighting it. You have fewer arguments and you are able to live peacefully, knowing that you can be understanding and friendly toward your fellow man.

Chapter 1 – January

Now let's try some affirmations for January. Each of these should be repeated on the day in question and the reason that you repeat the affirmations is so that your subconscious mind is led to believe what it is that you are saying. You must therefore say them with conviction and believe in the power of self-love to make them a part of your everyday life over the next 365 days.

Self-Love 365 Days

January affirmations – These are all about optimism for the coming year, but they are more than that. Your January affirmations help you get the year off to a great start that is positive and puts all of the negativity of the past behind you.

1. I am stronger than temptation
2. I am able to keep my promises to myself and others
3. I love who I am and excel in fulfilling my own expectations
4. I am warm inside and the cold winds cannot touch me
5. I share my warmth with friends and family
6. I am who I always intended to be
7. I am able to start the New Year with a positive outlook
8. I am rich beyond my dreams in good fortune
9. I believe in my abilities
10. I believe in my own powers of observation

Chapter 1 – January

11. I believe in God's grace as I walk through another winter's day

12. I believe in showing gratitude to everyone

13. I believe that humility is my strong point

14. I am able to give back to the world and do so gladly

15. I have a strength of character that is not questionable

16. I do good things every day of my life

17. My friends count on me to be their friend

18. I am happy and content that life allows me the privilege of being kind

19. My life is everything I ever wanted it to be

20. My days are spent in being happy with who I am

21. I move toward February with happiness in my heart

22. I am capable of doing anything I set my mind to

23. People know that they can count on me

Self-Love 365 Days

24. I rejoice in knowing that I can enjoy cold days in a warm home

25. I am grateful enough to thank my friends for the gifts they gave me at Christmas

26. I practice meditation every day

27. I am able to see beyond the obvious

28. My mind is at peace with who I am

29. My concentration levels are better than they ever have been

30. I am powerful enough to overcome anything

31. I have no doubts in who I am

If you say these affirmations and choose your order to suit your month of January, they all add up to positivity toward yourself, which results in self-love of a very beneficial kind. It sees the goodness in the world. It sees the goodness within you, but it does not ignore the potential weakness that everyone is prone to. It helps to build you up ready to face February with a smile and a happy heart.

Chapter 1 – January

January is a time of newness, with New Year's Day celebrations, and Martin Luther King Day. Add happiness to your February, but repeating the affirmations given above which apply to each day. You can take inspiration from them and allow them to become an important part of your first month of this year. Read through your daily affirmations and repeat them often on the day in question as this will help you to be able to embrace each idea that is laid out within the affirmations shown.

Chapter 2 – February

In February 2017, there are 28 days in the month. Not being a leap year, there is no need to worry about if someone will propose to you or whether you will initiate a proposal on the last day of the month that occurs only once every four years. Thus, you can make plans for the future year ahead and enjoy life as spring begins to show its promise to the world. With a full moon due on the 11th, you can expect to have some wonderfully detailed dreams, so make sure you go to bed early that night. As far as later in the month is concerned, be aware that there is a new moon on the 26th. This symbolizes your ability to put all your wishes and dreams into action, so it is particularly relevant to self-love affirmations. Those made at a time such as this should work toward aims and goals that you want to fulfill in the coming year.

Self-love is all about appreciating the gift of life that you have been given. It's about looking after yourself. It's also about making sure that you get sufficient food of the right kinds to provide the

Chapter 2 – February

nutrition that you need. It's also about getting sufficient sleep and learning to handle your stress levels. We told you about meditation in the last chapter. In this chapter, we want to talk about switching off negative thoughts. For this exercise, close your eyes and think of a time in your life that gave you a great deal of happiness. Picture it in your mind and see all the detail that you can muster because this is where you are going to go every time you think negative things over the next month. You will also be given a set of affirmations for this month – bearing in mind the changes in the moon and maximizing your potential.

Affirmations for February - Remember, the 11th of the month denotes dreamtime, while the 26th should be used to formulate dreams and ambitions. Use the phases of the moon to help to guide you in the kind of response you will get by using the following affirmation.

1. I love to see new buds starting on plants waking up from winter

2. I am thrilled that I have been given the ability to share happiness with others

3. I am rich in all things I need in order to fulfill my wildest dreams

4. I have no hang-ups about who I am

5. People trust my intuition and I am able to reassure them

6. I know that I have a very powerful ally in my inner voice

7. I have a wonderful life and enjoy every moment of it

8. There is nothing that I cannot do if I set my heart on it

9. I have dreams and ambitions and the character to work toward them

10. I love who I am because I represent the continuation of a family I love

11. I can make powerful choices in my life

12. I have the ability to make my own dreams come true

13. I have the intelligence to make choices that affect my life for the better

14. I enjoy performing small acts of kindness knowing they make people I love happy

Chapter 2 – February

15. I enjoy being myself and know my honesty is worthwhile holding onto

16. My focus in life is on self-love so I can give the best I am to those I love

17. I am healthier and younger at heart every day

18. I have a wonderful experience with money and can always make sufficient

19. I am able to give of myself but keep something back for me to love and appreciate

20. I am mindful of what other people need and happy to be part of their lives

21. I have a clear dream of what my life is and where it is going

22. I am able to follow the footsteps of my heart

23. I can achieve anything I set out to do because I know my own strengths

24. I understand my bodily needs for exercise and good food

Self-Love 365 Days

25. I choose to feel good about my life every day I live it

26. Nothing holds me back because I remove barriers by loving myself

27. I am blessed to be me and to have the great friendships I enjoy

28. I know that positivity is part of who I am

February is a time of celebration indeed with Valentine's Day being part of it as well as President's Day on the 20th of the month. If you don't have a Valentine, become your own Valentine. Send yourself a nice card to celebrate who you are. Don't forget others who may be feeling alone because a small gesture like sending them a card will help you feel better as well as making them feel loved. Sometimes people need that extra bit of input and if you are able to enjoy being you, help them to do the same.

Chapter 3 – March

In this month, everything is happening. The leaves are starting to form on the trees and it's beginning to feel like spring. The air is warmer and there's so much optimism in the air. It's a time of joyful celebration of life as everything that has been bleak for the winter period is coming to life. This is the time of year when you begin to see newborn lambs, although it's not yet time for thoughts of Easter.

In this month of self-love, you need to look at the negative influences in your life and start to distance yourself from them. Learning to live in the moment and embrace mindfulness helps you to concentrate on the now rather than disappointing relationships that may have left you emotionally scarred. The problem is that people develop self-esteem issues when those that are supposed to love them reject them. Self-loathing replaces self-love and that's very harmful to your psych. You need to step away from the harm done by the negative feedback you may have been given over the years. Other

Chapter 3 – March

people who influence the way you see yourself may include family members or your parents. People who don't love themselves are very much influenced by feedback. This is a month of renewal and it's time for the swan to come out of the egg and show the world the beauty that has remained obscured.

Let me tell you all about mindfulness. It means being able to switch off thoughts of the past at a moment's notice and pulling your mind back into the present moment. Try it. It will take a while before it's a habit, but when you do that, you switch negative thoughts for new thoughts and that's going to help you to love who you are, rather than live your life according to what other people said to you. Look around you. See all the goodness of the world and enjoy the moment you are in.

The affirmations for this month are all about self-development and belief in self. If you have come out of the other side of a relationship, you may actually find there are things about yourself you never knew existed. You may have found inner strength. You may have found yourself coping with things in a positive way. Keep positive because March brings out the part of you who is hidden away from the world and that person is valuable.

Self-Love 365 Days

Affirmations for March - There are 31 days in March and the new moon this month falls on the 12th of the month, while the new moon falls very late on, being on the night of the 27th and it's always worth keeping these dates in mind when using affirmations because they add power to them in a very positive way.

1. I am glad to be alive and to welcome the springtime in my life.

2. I am capable of shedding off the negativity of the past.

3. I walk through each day with my head held high.

4. My dreams are never limited and point me to true happiness

5. Today is the first day of the new me. Every day I renew who I am.

6. Miracles happen to me every day of my life

7. The budding plants in my garden need me as their friend

8. I smile at the world and know it will always smile back

Chapter 3 – March

9. My happiness is something I always invest in so I can share it with people I love

10. When I smile on the world, the sun shines

11. I am rich in love and able to do anything at all

12. I take care of what I eat and know my body is in great shape

13. Exercising is my way of saying thank you to my body for the service it does me

14. I do what I love doing because I can put all my heart into it

15. I am blessed with happiness each day of my life

16. Everyone who shares my life shares my positivity

17. I am energized and fit and ready to take on the world

18. I am wealthy right now, this moment

19. Everything comes easily to me because of my faith in me

20. I always share the beauty I see in others with them, so they see it too

21. I have no reason to seek love because I am it

22. I have perfect control over my life

23. I wake up in the morning with an attitude of gratitude

24. I look beyond the cover of a book and am eternally grateful for what I find

25. I do now allow myself to be limited by a narrow mind

26. If God smiles down, I catch the sunrays across my face.

27. There are so many ambitions I will fulfill this year

28. I can achieve creativity because I am created

29. There is optimism in every breath that I breathe

30. Faith in myself comes easily just as others are able to see I am worthy of believing in

Chapter 3 – March

31. Today, the sun shone on my life and I was grateful.

Bear in mind what you have learned about mindfulness as you go through this month because it helps you to maximize your experiences in life. When you are too stuck in the past or worried about tomorrow, you don't give yourself the space that you need to enjoy today. That's a waste of today because you should be embracing it and making the most of who you are in every moment of your life. Mindfulness makes your senses more aware and that, in turn, helps you to increase the positivity of your life.

Mindfulness also helps you to accept yourself. You get to enjoy being who you are because this moment allows that. When you dwell in the past, you let go of this potential opportunity.

Chapter 4 – April

This is the month of fools, but it doesn't have to include you! It's also the month that Easter takes place, as well as Americans celebrating Thomas Jefferson's birthday. What does this mean to you? It's the beginning of spring and a time when Easter eggs are in abundance and may tempt you to break one of those New Year resolutions you made as the year rolled in. Don't worry about that. A little indulgence in rich dark chocolate can really have positive effects instead of just an effect on your waistline.

In this month, you are getting ready to greet the sunshine. You have said goodbye to winter and all of the optimism of spring is in full force. You will feel lighter because you won't have to wrap up in so many clothes. You will have the odd day when it's warm enough to wear summer clothing and will certainly feel like you want to fulfill a load of things over the months that are to come. There's nothing to stop you. In fact, self-love includes a little self-indulgence sometimes and it

Chapter 4 – April

is this that helps you to feel whole and happy. Life isn't about possessions. It's about looking after yourself and you will find that this time of year is a great time to start treating yourself to a spa or a massage to help you feel your body is getting sculpted ready for the sunshine.

The affirmations for April will therefore include many, which relate to the way that others view you. Think of it as coming out of your shell and allowing your true self to shine.

April Affirmations – It's a time to come out of your shell and show yourself off to the world. The sun is shining and you are shedding layers getting ready for the summer. These affirmations will help you do so with panache.

1. I love the body I was born with and always look after it.

2. Getting out in the fresh air makes my body and mind happy and content

3. I am at total peace at this positive time of year

4. I believe in myself and am able to show that to people who want to confide in me.

5. People know who I am because I make no pretenses

6. I am authentic and love who I am because authenticity is everything

7. I am capable of handling my tasks with ease

8. I am unafraid of criticism because I know who I am and use it to learn from

9. I am able to accept my past and present because they all contribute to the positivity of who I am

10. I am excited to adapt to the changes of weather and season

11. I see who I am in the reflection of the way people view me.

12. I am positive in my approach and await the summer with optimism

13. I am a valuable part of the universe

14. My mind is able to create a tomorrow worth looking forward to

15. I know how to enjoy peace as it is part of who I am

Chapter 4 – April

16. I love to unwrap for the warm weather as I love the skin I am in

17. There is nothing to hold me back in life

18. I believe in my own ability to hold my hand out to greet honest friendship

19. I am able to make money easily

20. I enjoy the challenge of the seasons and embrace the changes

21. Everything that I need in life comes from within

22. I have discovered who I am and enjoy being me.

23. I love sleeping and allowing my mind to enjoy dreams that become realities

24. I am committed to learning and growing with each season that passes

25. I love those whose love is as sincere as mine

26. I am able to feel happiness because it's a constant state in my life

27. I never doubt my own abilities to be who I want to be

28. I love nature and learn from it the joy of being individual

29. I am proud of my body and the great shape it is in

30. I am able to see beyond the surface

All of these affirmations will help you to go forward in a positive way and repeated often will become your mantras. Loving yourself and believing in yourself are what help you to stand out from the crowd. They make you more compassionate, more understanding and happier with the way that your life is going. Remember that the world offers you a lot more than you know it can. As the days unfold, you can develop your dreams and make them your aims. By loving yourself and believing in all possibilities, life opens new doors to you all the time. Be ready to open them and get as much happiness out of being you as is possible.

Chapter 5 – May

It's apple blossom time. The cherry blossom also shows at its best in this month. With Mother's Day and Memorial Day falling in May, you are already aware of caring and how important your caring is both for the mom that you love and for keeping thoughts alive of those who have passed. In May, the full moon falls on the 10th while the full moon happens toward the end of the month. On this particular month, when your body is getting more natural vitamins from the sun, it's time to look at the way in which you deal with problems that you see other people as having caused. Learning all about compassion and empathy will be your self-love tasks for the month. When someone upsets you, instead of thinking negative thoughts, place yourself in that person's shoes and learn to enhance your level of understanding. You will then see yourself as a much more positive kind of person than one who retorts with negative words. Try to imagine what it's like for people who live on drama because they don't know any other way to be. Be compassionate and show by example that drama

Chapter 5 – May

isn't necessary. All people need to be is who they are. Teach friends that you don't measure them by what they own but by who they are in your life.

If you start to become more compassionate and empathetic, you give yourself more to love about yourself. It isn't vain love. It's love that you learn to embrace because you know that your own compassion and empathy make you feel better about who you are. People who speak badly to others usually feel bad about who they are. I have often told people that insults reflect upon the person who speaks them rather than on the person to whom those insults are directed. Take this kind of activity out of your life and see the bigger picture because when you do, you will love who you are more. In this month, make a note to get in touch with people who reinforce your value. You may have been out of touch for a while with positive friends. Try to learn to say "no" to those friends who use you because being used can make you feel less important than you actually are. You need to decide between toxic friends – who use all your energy and give nothing in return – and those friends who are always supportive. When you phone up old friends, make the call about that person rather than about you. That way, you are learning active listening and empathy and that's vital to the self-love equation.

Affirmations for May – These bear in mind what we have spoken about above and will help you to be more empathetic and understanding, thus increasing your value to other people.

1. I am the best friend anyone could ever have.
2. I listen and give importance to what friends are saying.
3. I value friendships and know that I deserve them.
4. I easily show my empathy toward others
5. I can step into the shoes of someone else and see their world as clearly as my own.
6. I always know the right thing to say
7. I am good at active listening and people love me for it
8. I can help people through their stresses without making demands
9. I am well known for being a caring human being

Chapter 5 – May

10. I am compassionate and caring

11. Caring comes naturally to me

12. I know how to be sensitive when sensitivity is called for

13. I do not exercise anger and there is no room for negativity in my life

14. I have dropped the dead wood of my life and gathered good friendships

15. I am able to recognize the qualities of good friendship because I am one.

16. I enjoy being empathetic because it makes me more open minded

17. I know that my problems are small and manageable

18. I am able to listen to others and help them to see life more clearly

19. I never need to worry about emotional support

20. I am emotionally strong and able to give so much love

Self-Love 365 Days

21. I have learned that I am stronger than I ever thought possible

22. I understand people and it is this understanding that makes me whole

23. There are never times when I am too tired to listen

24. I will never be a doormat to toxic people

25. I can recognize good friendships and encourage them

26. My empathy levels have increased with practice

27. Empathy is second nature to me.

28. I understand my own failings and these make me stronger

29. I keep in touch with people who matter to me

30. I am strong and capable of self-love as well as love for others

31. I like what I have to offer friends and look for those same qualities in others.

Chapter 5 – May

All of these affirmations are geared around friendships and recognizing those that are of value in life and those that need to be put aside.

Chapter 6 – June

June is the month to remember Fathers. It's also one when the full moon happens on the 9th and the new moon on the 23rd of the month. It's a time when all the flowers come out and the garden looks beautiful, even though the hard work of gardening comes into its own. It's a time to think of creation. In this month, it's great to get out in the fresh air and enjoy the world. The trees are in leaf and everything is new and fresh.

This may also be a good month to practice relaxation. When you are able to relax, you lose an element of stress from your life and are able to think things through in such a fashion that you feel in control of your life. You are able to sleep well and feel good about life. Self-love means looking after yourself. Sleep and relaxation are an important part of that care. This exercise will help you to be able to relax and then when things get difficult, you can escape into your own area and relax instead of stressing that you may be doing something wrong. You

Chapter 6 – June

need relaxation to help you to get the world back into perspective.

To relax, lie down on your bed and use only one pillow. This enables your airways to be clear. Lie on your back and place your arms beside you. Wear comfortable clothing and make sure that the room is warm. Close your eyes and think of your toes. Tense them and be aware of them tensing. Then relax them until they feel heavy. Relaxation works because it lowers your blood pressure and helps you to restore natural balance in your life. It energizes you and makes your heart healthier. Now think of the next part of the body and go through the same process. Flex it and then relax it. During the course of your relaxation, concentrate on the parts of the body and upon your breathing and if you start to have anxious thoughts about anything else at all, dismiss those thoughts. Concentrate on relaxing the entire body, from the soles of your feet, right up to the top of your head. When you have finished, relax for a moment before going back to your normal pace of life. This is important, so that your heart can begin to increase in beating and your blood pressure can return to normal.

Affirmations for June – These affirmations are all about self-care. This is the care needed in order to love yourself and to make the best of who you are.

1. I can feel my body relax and my breathing sustain me.
2. I love my life and the amount of relaxation it gives me.
3. I am able to relax at will and use this to control my emotions.
4. I can gain energy from relaxing every day
5. My mind is slowing down ready for sleep
6. I know that I am centered and my life is balanced
7. My muscles are relaxed
8. Every time I practice relaxation, I become stronger and more energetic
9. My mind is relaxed and my breathing is strong
10. I am able to gain impetus from simply learning to be still

Chapter 6 – June

11. Relaxing is becoming easier and easier every day

12. I give my body the relaxation and exercise that it needs

13. My mind is at perfect peace

14. Relaxing my body is my way to fill my life with energy

15. I have a natural ability to switch off and relax

16. I enjoy the pleasure of deep relaxation

17. I know my body appreciates relaxing sometimes

18. The relaxation I impose on myself makes me stronger

19. I know that each time I lay down to sleep, sleep will come

20. I put my worries away at night and make sleep a vacation

21. Letting go of tension and strain helps to make me strong

22. I know that I am a valuable person

23. I allow relaxing music to alter negative moods

24. My positivity comes from being able to switch off

25. I can go through life with happiness because I give myself sufficient relaxation

26. I am more active because I care more about balancing my life

27. I transform my body to being centered every time I relax

28. I know that my mind is peaceful and calm

29. I can close my eyes and visualize my future

30. I have no doubts about my own ability to relax.

All of these affirmations are written to help you to accept that relaxation should be a part of your everyday life. If you find that it isn't, these affirmations will help you to see the importance of relaxation.

Chapter 7 – July

Since July encompasses Independence Day, it may be a good time to think of your own independence. In this month, the affirmations that are going to be suggested center around how important it is to self-love that you see yourself as a whole person. I say this because many people believe they would be nothing without their partner. This isn't strictly true unless you have self-esteem issues. You are an independent person from your partner but that doesn't mean you love your partner less. It simply means that you have more to offer him/her.

You cannot be measured by who loves you or who you have in your life. You have to understand that the reason you are loved is because you are a complete person and if you offered your partner less than that, you need to look at ways to love yourself more and become more complete so that you offer your partner the maximum that you are able to. You wouldn't buy a toy that depended upon another toy to make it

Chapter 7 – July

viable. It wouldn't make sense and would make the initial purchase a little bit questionable. Therefore, why should you think that your partner should accept you if you are inferior in some way or have something lacking? Self-love allows you to see yourself as the whole person that you are.

Never confuse self-love with selfishness. It is a totally different concept. Self-love means you accept who you are and actually enjoy being that person. You don't need to bend and change all the time to suit others because they chose you because of who you are. Be proud of that and enjoy all the benefits that self-love gives you. Be confident. You won't be confident in everything because no one is. You should also have independent interests and things that you love doing on your own. This month is all about YOU and facing up to the fact that you are independent. It's healthy that you are and helps to make you more of a complete package.

July Affirmations – These are all about independence and what better time to express them? Within the affirmations for July, you will find you have a voice and are entitled to it.

1. I have a wonderful sense of appreciation of music

2. I am able to appreciate art for what it is

3. I love being creative and excel in it

4. I am able to create ideas on paper and write my emotions down

5. Being creative is my greatest joy in life

6. I enjoy being on my own as I am good company

7. I embrace the creativity that I have in my soul

8. I enjoy company although have no need of it all of the time

9. I enjoy doing things on my own

10. I know that life offers me many opportunities to shine as an individual

11. I depend on no one and am self-sufficient

Chapter 7 – July

12. I love who I am and enjoy waking up each day

13. My life is enhanced by my friendships although my friendship with myself is of paramount importance

14. I am my own best friend and know all my secrets

15. I enjoy being alone as it gives me a chance to be me

16. I live life on my own terms and am happy with them

17. I am proud to be my own person

18. I have self-confidence and people admire me for it

19. I am able to think independently

20. I see clearly my own image of the future

21. I am able to face problems head on

22. I am not afraid of difficult situations and can turn them around

23. Each day of my life, I celebrate my independence

24. I am a whole person and others compliment me for it

25. I am able to walk into a room alone and not feel lonely

26. I observe life sometimes and see a very independent person when I look in the mirror

27. I am capable of doing anything I set my heart to

28. I am entitled to have my own tastes and choices in life

29. I can enjoy sharing my choices with others

30. I make myself whole by loving who I am

31. I know that I was created as a whole person

If you have problems with your independence, you can carry these affirmations with you for more than the month and continue to repeat them to help you to gain independence.

Chapter 8 – August

August brings out the sunshine and it's time to get out and about and enjoy yourself. One of the best ways to feel good about yourself is to go to places that inspire you. These are beauty spots, which give you that feeling that you are not on your own in life.

Amid all the splendor of the scenery, you are reminded that no matter how small you are, your place in this world is every bit as important. Imagine a beach with no grains of sand or a pebbly foreshore with no pebbles. You are an important link to nature and getting out and about in this month will help you to feel the benefit of the sunshine and to embrace the world that you live in:

Chapter 8 – August

Affirmations for August – These are all about celebration of life.

1. I am talented and strong and able to feel complete happiness

2. I love nature and it inspires me to be a better person

3. I know that the whole world lies before me and I am ready to take on the challenge.

4. I love my life and the sunshine of August helps me to see it more clearly

5. I celebrate my life by sharing time with natural environments

Self-Love 365 Days

6. I know that my strength comes from my weakness for the wonders of this world

7. When I take the time to meditate upon life, it enriches me

8. I have everything I want in life and could never ask for more

9. There is no price anyone could pay that equals my happiness and contentment

10. My awareness of the present moment enhances my life no end

11. I am able to allow the sunshine to caress my soul and feel its warmth

12. I am nearer to my God when I am in a naturally beautiful environment

13. The sun always shines on my life

14. There are no gray clouds in my life, only opportunities waiting to happen

15. I can see beyond the rainbow to where skies are blue

16. The morning dew wakes me and makes me feel alive

Chapter 8 – August

17. The photo opportunities of the summer capture the greatness of my life

18. I am with friends, though remain true to myself at all times

19. I can look into the sunny garden and enjoy nature to its fullest

20. There has never been a better time to celebrate being me

21. I know that there are cloudy days, but they never cloud my judgment

22. There are so many victories in my life

23. I know that I am a winner when I see the world I live in

24. I see the first changing of color in the leaves and celebrate the gold nature gives me

25. I can see beyond all material possessions to a richer place

26. I am happy with my thoughts and even happier with my deeds

27. Summer brings out the swan and allows it to swim

28. I am grateful for the abundance in my life

29. The abundance in my life continues to sustain me

30. Those who do not love themselves can only understand me when they learn to embrace their lives

31. I mix with positive people who celebrate my life as well as celebrating their own.

All of these affirmations are about celebration and can be used in other months, such as that of your birthday. If you want to make the most of being you, treat yourself to a trip to a place where you can see the true splendor of the world. Perhaps you can have a vacation at the beach. Perhaps you can see places far away or even start to appreciate those closer to home. There are loads of opportunities in this month because the sun is shining.

This is also a month that is filled with optimism. Make the most of it and ensure that you feel at one with nature as well as with yourself. Wear a flower in your hair if you are a woman or simply enjoy the color of the plants in the park because they are there to remind you what a rich and rewarding world you live in.

Chapter 9 – September

September 4th is Labor Day and a day of celebration. Let's look at ways in which you can love what you do for a living. The people that you mix with at work will form a large part of your life. When they know that you are a self-loving and confident person, you will find that many will come to you when they need advice and help. Be generous with your time and realize that it's a compliment that people respect who you are.

This month is all about work. What do you do for a living? How can you bring self-love into the workplace? Self-love should follow you wherever you go and be a part of your life, regardless of the people you mix with or the duties that you have to perform.

Chapter 9 – September

Affirmations for September – These center upon study and work related issues and will help you to be calm and strong in the workplace or in your following of new studies.

1. I am very focused and am able to think clearly

2. I know what I want in life and am actively pursuing it

3. I love myself unconditionally and this shows in my work

4. I am able to earn a living doing what I love

5. I know that learning is something I thrive on

6. I am able to learn easily and learn new systems rapidly

7. I am always helpful to my fellow colleagues

8. My work gives me a sense of self

9. I love the way that work helps me feel good about myself

10. It doesn't matter how mundane the work. I make it shine.

11. My attitude toward work is unquestionably sincere

12. I am able to give to others less talented because it's part of who I am

13. I never mind other people's anger because I manage anger so well

14. I am never negative at work.

15. I love the way that people are drawn toward me for help

16. I radiate happiness

17. Things always work out for me with ease

Chapter 9 – September

18. I share my time with others less fortunate than myself

19. I am forever grateful for being born with a generous soul

20. I know that I am a product of my own actions

21. My actions toward others are positive and encouraging

22. I always stay calm in moments of crisis

23. I am able to distinguish the difference between thoughtful reflection and stress

24. My work makes a difference to the world I live in

25. I am going to have the best day ever today

26. I am strong when tackling problems head on

27. I know that I learn easily and can absorb information fast

28. I am not afraid of technology and am always thrilled to learn

29. Yes, I can.

30. I am perfect exactly the way that I am

Use these affirmations in the workplace and stick to them. They will help you to accept difficult situations and work through them. They will also help your happiness levels. You are a wonderful human being and in your contact with other people, need to remember that. Interact in a positive way and enjoy that interaction. Smile at the world and watch as it smiles back. You deserve it and when you make the most of this kind of opportunity, you really do make work seem like a breeze.

Chapter 10 – October

In October, the leaves are beginning to come down from the trees, but there are still loads of sunny days. Make the most of this time to stock up on Vitamin D from the sun and enjoy the colors of fall.

Chapter 10 – October

October Affirmations – These affirmations are all about renewal. This is the time of year when the world slows down for the autumnal period and you will need extra energy to get you through the colder times.

1. Today I choose to encounter the spiritual side of my nature.

2. I am at one with the earth and can enjoy the golds of autumn

3. I am rich in experiences and love my life

4. Each moment, I breathe in the breath of life and feel gratitude

5. I am grateful for the renewal of the earth's store of good things for the coming season.

6. I enjoy life to the fullest and am not afraid of moving forward

7. I can meditate upon the earth's bountiful nature

8. Every moment given to me is a fresh opportunity to experience self-love

9. Self-love enables me to feel in harmony with nature

10. I enjoy the warmth of a wonderful fire inside my heart

11. I have learned that all my problems resolve themselves

12. I love the life that I have been given as a gift from my maker

13. Every single day, I wake up happy to be me

14. I walk in the forest and feel God's love surround me

15. There are always days when the skies are sad though there is no darkness in my heart.

16. I know the path that my life is taking and am happy with it

17. I can share love with people around me through being conscious of self-love

18. I wake up knowing that a new day greets me that is better than yesterday

19. I am aware of my strengths and use them to support me through times of weakness

Chapter 10 – October

20. There is no time to feel sorry for myself, but eternally grateful for the world I was born into

21. I see my face in a puddle and the reflection fills me with happiness

22. There is nothing I cannot do in my life

23. I know how lucky I am in my life and seem to attract good things

24. I am able to see the good in all people

25. I am eternally grateful for the optimism that is part of who I am

26. I know that darkness cannot stop the light that burns inside me

27. The evenings may be coming sooner, but the warmth of my heart stays the same.

28. I am happy with the amount of love I feel inside me.

29. My meditation helps me to keep my life on track.

30. I am going places in my life and my happiness soars with the passing of time.

Perhaps it's also worth keeping the last affirmation for Halloween!

31. I am never afraid of ghosts or things that go bump in the night.

Chapter 11 - November

Of course, this is a month of Thanksgiving, a time when we should all be grateful, but gratitude serves more purpose than just being something to feel on one day a year. The more grateful you are for all the things in your life, the less likely you are to feel bad things about yourself. People who self-love have the compassion to know when others have added to their lives and their thanks to these people should be something that is thought about all the year round. November is also a month when our Veterans are remembered with love for all that they have done to help make our country a greater place. Thus, some of the affirmations made in this month will reflect that.

Chapter 11 - November

November Affirmations – These are affirmations of thanks to go with Thanksgiving. They are also affirmations that will help lead you up to the last month of the year, thinking about what you feel about family and friendships.

1. I am grateful to have such a wonderful family.

2. I am forever grateful to all the veterans who have made this world a better place to be.

3. I will always walk forward in my life knowing that I have much to be thankful for.

4. I am always thankful for the help and support of my family.

5. I am what I think and therefore keep my thoughts pure and positive

6. I am the builder of my life and make sure it has a solid foundation

7. I am overflowing with joy because my love is enough for everyone

8. I am better than negative actions can ever be

9. I put myself on a par with positivity and see it as who I am

10. I find forgiveness easy and this makes me more compassionate

11. Forgiving those who make mistakes makes me more complete

12. My relationship with others is strengthened by my love

13. I possess the right qualities for complete happiness

14. I am grateful to my family for all of their love

15. I know that I have inherited my mother's compassion

Chapter 11 - November

16. I am complete because I know and love who I am

17. I choose happiness through being loving and kind

18. I am fortunate to have many brave people in my life as examples

19. I am courageous enough to stand by my convictions

20. Believing in good, I can walk among kinds or paupers

21. I am successful in life because I appreciate those who sacrificed to give me the love I needed in order to grow

22. I abandon old habits daily and put positive ones in their place.

23. I am indestructible, because true love cannot be stifled

24. I love those around me, though know my own self-love to be the love I can truly depend upon

25. My future lies before me because I have the power to plan it

26. I radiate all things that are good and whole.

27. I am grateful for my family and their example.

28. I wake up each day with clarity in my mind

29. I am able to dream and allow my dreams to come to fruition

30. I am at peace with all the events in my life and all which will come to pass

November is indeed a month of gratitude and when you can find a list of things to be grateful for each day of the month, you also find that your life is filled to brimming with positivity and happiness.

Chapter 12 – December

The years roll by and December always brings a month of giving. It's also a time to remember all about people you care about. Ahead of you this month, you have all the celebrations, the meals, the parties and the potential of making new resolutions for the New Year. However, you also have the wonder of a choir singing holy songs and filling the atmosphere with that warmth we know as Christmas. This month is all about giving and about planning.

Chapter 12 – December

December Affirmations – Planning ahead for the New Year and making plans to be with people you love is all part and parcel of the December experience.

1. My plans to be happy this December will happen just as I thought they would.

2. I am able to give part of who I am to all those who I love

3. I know that the gifts I make with my hands I give with my heart

4. I can share celebrations with close ones and give boxes filled with happiness

5. My plans for the New Year are always a success because I have faith in myself

6. I am filled with the light of Christmas and share it with friends and family

7. The joy of the season fills my heart to bursting

8. Christmas is a time for giving and that suits who I am

9. I give part of me to all who love me this Christmas

10. I am complete in my knowledge that God's grace follows me

11. Christmas gives me license to share all the love I have inside

12. I am committed to remaining happy throughout the holidays

13. I know that my resolutions will be sensible ones as I trust my judgment

14. I am happy to see a New Year in with hope in my heart

15. I am positive and happy with all the choices I make in life

16. I give with love, though keep enough love left inside for me

17. The strength of my character gets me through difficult family situations

18. I give with all my heart but have learned that giving doesn't count the cost

19. I am strong in character and have enough love to share with strangers

20. The sights and sounds of Christmas choirs fill me with a warm glow

Chapter 12 – December

21. I love to heard carols being sung and feel them warm my heart

22. I am a capable person and love my strength of character

23. I love the people around me but the strength of love comes from within

24. Christmas is in every breath that I take

25. I meditate on the wonders of Christmas and feel its joy

26. I never feel guilt at Christmas because I feel love all the year around

27. Christmas is a time of giving without guilt or expectation

28. I am strong in my resolve to be generous and kind

29. I love to see the fairy lights glow out their warmth

30. I am a valuable human being and each Christmas confirms this

31. All of the New Year resolutions I make tonight will help me to love myself and others more.

And so, we come to the end of the year and it's time to look over how all of these self-love affirmations have changed the way that we view life.

Conclusion

For next year, you can modify the affirmations and work on your weak points. For example, if you have problems with independence, work on those affirmations and make yourself stronger. If the world is moving too fast, look back on the chapter that deals with meditation or the relaxation chapter, as these will all help you to gain back that self-love you should be feeling. Stresses and strains in life can sometimes take the spotlight off self-love. However, it's the very basis of your existence and should be there at all times to help strengthen your character to be able to deal with the many occasions that life will throw at it.

It is hoped that you have enjoyed this 365 days of affirmations and that you will look out for future editions. Self-love is all about acceptance. It's all about compassion and the ability to empathize. Think about people that you know and love and ask yourself what qualities you admire in those people. Then work out how you can incorporate those things into your own life. It's nothing to do

Conclusion

with outward appearance. It's all to do with the spirit of the person and that's something you can work on and get to love. Your own adaptation of ideas and ideals you gain from the heroes of your life will help you to go through life with complete love for self and respect that will make you a very strong person for others to love and depend upon.

We have already stressed the importance of individuality. You are an island. We all are regardless of whether we are in relationships or not. The wholeness of your individual self is what makes you comfortable with your inner child. Make sure that you increase your knowledge by reading on a regular basis. Be up to date with what's going on in your world and be aware that you need to look after yourself and keep yourself safe. When you feel stressed, go back to the chapter on relaxation and re-affirm the ideas that were contained therein. Re-exercise yourself in relaxation and try to build this into your stressful life, so that the person inside is kept strong against a tide of anxiety and pressure. Once you do incorporate sufficient relaxation into your life, you will find that your own inner strength develops to such an extent that you can carry on loving who you are, even when the chips are down.

Happy New Year and may all your dreams for the coming year become realities.

If you like to keep stay in touch or stay up to date for promotion/ upcoming books.

Please join our publisher facebook page : https://www.facebook.com/surprisepublishing/

Thank you so much and welcome to our family

Made in the USA
Columbia, SC
09 August 2019